Austin

Austin

An American Extreme Bull Riders Tour Romance

Jeannie Watt

TULE
PUBLISHING

Austin

ISBN: 978-1-947636-16-3

Dedication

This story is dedicated to Jamie Dallas, my favorite critique partner. I appreciate you letting me bounce ideas off you, and for pointing out the stuff I don't see. Whenever I write myself into a corner, I know I'll be okay because you're there. Thank you!

Chapter One

"THIS IS MY last stop for the night." Austin Harding had downed most of his alcohol quota at the American Extreme Bull Riders sponsors' party that evening, then had one more for the road when he and his fellow bull riders stopped at a dive bar while walking back to the high-rise Reno casino where they were staying. He needed to get back to his hotel room sometime before dawn, ice his shoulder and hip and look at video of the bull he'd drawn for the prelims.

"You said that at the last place," Gustavo Santos pointed out, his words trailing off as a waitress passed by wearing a modernized version of a saloon girl costume. A fluffy curled feather bobbed on the back of her head, and the black and red dress she wore was cut low at the top and short at the bottom, leaving little to the imagination.

Okay. Maybe one last drink hadn't been a terrible idea.

"Over there." T.J. Casey pointed to an empty table in the far corner. "And I'm with Austin. Last stop, Gus."

"Yeah, yeah, yeah." Gus turned his dark eyes toward the new guy, Josh McIntosh, who'd just qualified for the top tier

1

of the tour, as they made their way through the crowd to the table. "How about you, *mano*?"

Josh shrugged as they sat down. "I'll play it by ear."

"You'll regret those words when you wake up in some strange place in the morning," Austin said. Gus was a great guy and a hell of a bull rider, but he wasn't good about practicing moderation in any area of his life.

A coaster with the casino logo appeared in front of him a few seconds later, and he automatically glanced up at the waitress, who was standing so close that he couldn't get a good look at her.

"What can I get you guys?"

A memory stirred at the sound of her voice, but Austin couldn't pin it down. He craned his neck to get a better look, but the angle wasn't good. Creamy skin, long reddish-brown hair. High cheekbones, full lips. All somehow familiar, even at the awkward angle. The woman stayed stubbornly close to him, her satin skirt brushing against his arm as she took Gage, Casey and Gustavo's orders.

"And you?"

That voice…

Well, shit.

He moved his chair back so he could get a good look at the woman. "Kristen?"

She looked behind her, as if expecting to find a woman named Kristen standing there, then turned back so that he could see her face. She *looked* like Kristen Alexander, but her hair was longer and her expression was blank. No hint of recognition. "I'm sorry?"

Austin frowned more deeply as he studied her. Maybe he was wrong…but he didn't think so.

"You aren't from Montana?" *You didn't rip me to shreds in front of a crowd at Marietta High School?*

The woman's fingers tightened on her tray as she lifted her eyebrows in a cool expression. "Sorry. No. What would you like?"

He frowned at her, but her expression didn't change. "Jameson. Neat."

She turned without another word and headed back to the bar, stopping at tables on the way to check on her customers.

"What was that about?"

"Nothing." Austin turned his attention back to Casey, but continued to watch the waitress over the bull rider's shoulder. "She looks like someone I knew once."

The idea of Kristen Alexander—the woman who'd told him she wouldn't be seen with him because he was a loser—schlepping drinks in a bar bordered on being crazy. The last he'd heard from her twin, Whitney, Kristen was conquering the world of high finance, but Whit hadn't mentioned the city where her sister was doing said conquering.

Could that city be Reno?

Even if it was, people who conquered financial worlds during the day didn't normally moonlight in casino bars at night. Hell, Kristen hadn't partied even a little during high school. Hadn't done anything that wasn't directly related to some sort of an achievement. The woman collected awards the way other people collected loose change. The idea of her willingly putting on the saloon girl getup, hanging her tits out there for everyone to see, was ridiculous. Austin kicked back in his chair and told himself he was nuts. That woman couldn't be Kristen.

But she sure as hell looked like her.

The discussion segued into bulls as they waited for their drinks. The good, the bad, the ugly. The un-rideable. They were deep into a debate as to which bull was the most dangerous on the circuit when the waitress reappeared and started setting drinks on the table. A Budweiser near Cody's elbow, the double shot of Jameson next to his. Austin glanced up.

"Are you sure you're not from Montana?"

Color rose in the woman's cheeks as her expression went stony in the exact same way Kristen Alexander's used to—except for the time he'd tipped her over. Then she'd been anything but stone-like. "I'm from a small town in Nevada."

"Yeah?" Austin smiled a little. "Which one?"

"Tonopah."

He gave a short nod. "Go to high school there?"

"I did." She looked as if she wanted to be anywhere except where she was. Why?

"I forget…what's Tonopah's mascot?"

The waitress stilled. "Excuse me?"

"The high school mascot. What is it?"

She swallowed. Her mouth opened, closed again, then she blurted, "It's a rattlesnake." Her gaze drilled into his, as if daring him to question her further.

He was done.

Cody lifted his glass. "Now that's a mascot. Mine was a—"

"Chipmunk?" Austin asked.

"Fuck you."

The Kristen-look-alike took advantage of the moment to slip away. All for the best, really. Austin didn't need a mystery or anything else to screw with his focus. So what if their waitress was the spitting image of the girl who'd ripped him to shreds in front of a crowd? It had been years ago. He gave her one final farewell look over his shoulder as she walked away, then sat up straighter as he spotted the scar just above her right elbow.

Son of a bitch.

He knew that scar—had studied it during math class when he'd sat behind Kristen Alexander and spent more time focused on her than on what the instructor was blathering on about. He'd even asked her about it, thinking that maybe she'd talk to him.

No way.

His eyes narrowed as Kristen—it had to be her—edged her way past a group of women wearing dresses that were too tight and heels that were too high. In other words, damned hot women. Likely Josh would have one of them in a convenient bathroom stall soon.

"Are you up to it?" Gus asked, obviously referring to the women, not Kristen, who was now at the bar.

Austin settled back in his chair, lifted his drink. "I am…but I won't."

Gus coughed into his fist, but Austin ignored him as he sipped the Jameson. What was Kristen Alexander, the woman who'd told *him* that *he* was going nowhere in life, doing working in a mid-level casino?

He pulled out his phone, but before he could look up the Tonopah mascot, Casey said, "You know what? She lied to you." He held out his phone to show Austin a cartoon prospector.

"No shit." He sipped again. "I think she just wanted to get rid of me."

Casey gave a small snort. "Makes sense. I'd like to get rid of you, too, at times."

"Ah…you know you love me."

Casey tipped back his beer while Austin once again zeroed in on Kristen, who was checking tables on the opposite side of the room.

He wasn't the vengeful type…not usually. But this situation was different, and he felt as if it needed to be addressed. Now. While he had the opportunity.

Guess what, Kris? The roosters have come home to roost.

SOMEHOW KRISTEN MANAGED not to hyperventilate on the long walk back to the bar. She'd just about died when Austin Harding and his friends came into the casino bar and sat in her section. What were the chances of someone from back home ending up in the Silver Bow Casino? And of all people, Austin Harding? Really?

But she survived. Barely. When she chanced a look at the table of bull riders, they were deep in conversation. As far as she could tell, squinting across the dimly lit room while trying to appear as if she wasn't staring, not one of them had a phone out to look up the real mascot of Tonopah, Nevada. Maybe she'd guessed correctly? Surely some school in Nevada had a rattlesnake as a mascot—why not Tonopah?

She kept an eye on Austin's table from a distance. She had to go back eventually. Check on them.

Although…maybe no one would notice if she didn't?

It'd been crazy to pretend she didn't know Austin, crazier still to have gotten away with it. It would be *beyond* crazy to push things—and maybe she didn't have to. Her manager was busy with the private party. Jess and Christa, the bartenders, were slammed. She could stay 'busy' elsewhere.

Which was exactly what she did, feeling shifty the entire time. To her utter relief, the guys stood after only one round and started dropping money on the table. Bullet dodged. Or so she thought until Eva, the head waitress, cruised up to where she was waiting for an order at the end of the bar.

"Are you allergic to cowboys or something?" Before Kristen could speak, Eva gave her an accusing look. "I don't think they would have left so early if you'd gone back to check on them. You know…done your job?"

Kristen's cheeks warmed, because she rarely if ever slacked, but tonight she had. For a very good reason.

"I…" She met Eva's cold gaze and the words petered out.

"Do better," Eva said flatly.

"I will." The tips were shared communally and if someone slacked, everyone suffered. She didn't want that—but she also didn't want Austin telling people back home in Marietta that she was working in a casino instead of sitting in her cubicle crunching numbers…like her family thought she was.

Point made, Eva turned away and started rattling off a list of drinks to Christa, who lined up glasses.

After her shift ended, Kristen kicked off the bootie shoes that were part of her western saloon girl costume and peeled off the fishnet stockings. After checking her feet for blood—there was none—she shoved the killer hosiery into her bag, slid her feet into her blessedly roomy flats, picked up the bootie shoes and headed out of the staff room, still feeling keyed up from her near miss with Austin. But it was over. She was safe.

"See you," she said to Deke, the security guy, as she passed by his office on the way down the narrow hall leading to the exit. He gave a small grunt, keeping his focus on the cameras that covered the parking lot and the surrounding areas. Taciturn habits aside, Deke seemed like a good guy—just very quiet and focused on his job. She understood quiet and focused—it was the strategy she'd used for years to insulate herself from situations she didn't know how to handle. Keep your mouth shut; look like you know what you're doing. Take no chances and let Whitney run the show.

Her strategy had worked fine in high school, where she'd had her twin to run interference and a few close friends. Not so fine in college, where people assumed that someone who did as well as she did academically, yet rarely spoke, had to be stuck up.

No…not stuck up. Just anxious and very adept at hiding it. Like it or not, she had the ice princess thing down pat.

Her mouth twisted as she shoved the thought out of her head. She wasn't going there. Not again. The thing was, she wasn't any wimpier than Whit when push came to shove. She was simply more tuned in to what other people thought. Less likely to make a scene. And harder on herself.

In a lot of ways, serving drinks at the Silver Bow was good for her. She was forced to interact with a multitude of people and every day she worked on faking a higher level of comfort than she felt. It was working. She was less flustered every day, but that didn't keep her from longing for her old world. The one where she could disappear into her cubicle and immerse herself in a project. Take the kind of risks she was comfortable with. Academic ones.

Kristen pushed the heavy metal door open and stepped out into the parking lot, thankful that it was so well lit. Her roommate's tiny Ford Escort was parked only a few spaces away from the entrance, and she started toward it when the door behind her opened and an unexpected voice stopped her in her tracks.

"It's not a rattlesnake, you know."

Kristen whirled around as Austin stepped out of the building a few feet behind her, letting the door swing shut behind him. "The Tonopah mascot," he clarified. "Not a rattlesnake."

Kristen pressed a hand to her chest, trying to keep her heart from beating its way out. "You startled me."

One corner of Austin's mouth lifted, not in a particularly friendly way, and then he pulled his phone out of his pocket, brought up a screen and held it out. The picture was difficult to make out from a few yards away, but it appeared to be a cartoon man wielding a pickax and shovel.

"What is that?" Kristen asked, her voice little more than a husky whisper.

"*That* is a mucker."

A mucker. "Tonopah's mascot?"

"Uh-huh." Austin dropped the phone back into his pocket, then folded his arms over his chest, making his shoulder muscles ripple under his cotton cowboy shirt.

"What gives, Kris?"

"I'm sorry." The apology tumbled out as she tried to make her brain work. She was in a spot, but maybe she could talk her way out of it. All she had to do was tell the truth, ask for cooperation…from the guy she'd cut down in front of his friends years ago. She'd been justified, but she hadn't been kind, and she still cringed at the memory of what had gone down between them.

"You're sorry," he said flatly, a note of incredulity in his voice.

"I am." The words were inadequate, but what else could she say?

Austin's eyes narrowed. "What are you sorry about, Kris? That you lied to me? Or that I caught you in the lie?"

Kristen cleared her throat. This is where the talking part came in, where she cajoled him into understanding her situation—but her brain was not cooperating and as the uncomfortable seconds ticked by, she felt herself withdrawing into self-protection mode, shutting down, clamming up. Her curse.

"Your family doesn't know that you're working here, do they?" He held her gaze, waiting for her response, his expression hard. She'd forgotten how blue his eyes were. Piercing blue. Pirate blue.

Going to cause her a world of trouble blue.

"No." She finally found her voice to confess. "They don't know."

Once again, the corner of his amazing mouth tilted up. Damn but she'd fantasized about that mouth in high school—although she'd been too self-conscious to ever let anyone know. Not even her twin.

"I figured if they were aware, I would have heard about it from Whitney the last time we spoke—which wasn't that long ago." He gave a short, harsh laugh as he tipped his head back to take in the garish neon sign on the rear of the old brick building blinking on and off above Kristen's head. "I guess I could say something about how the mighty have fallen."

She opened her mouth, determined to force some words out, to start her plea for understanding, when the door squeaked open behind her. Deke stepped out into the parking lot, rolling his shoulders before coming to a stop.

"You okay?" he asked Kristen without looking away from Austin, who seemed less than impressed with the security man's bulk.

"I am," she murmured. Or she would be, once she managed to square things with Austin, explain herself. Ask him not to tell her family, that she hadn't told them everything going on in her life. Hadn't wanted to add to their stress. Hadn't wanted to admit that in a way she was a loser.

Austin touched his hat at Deke in a respectful way. "I was just going."

Kristen's eyes went wide. He couldn't go. They weren't done. "I'll give you a ride." The words blurted out on a note of desperation.

"No thanks." He gave her a curt nod and headed off across the parking lot toward the street, favoring one leg ever so slightly. If Deke hadn't been there, she would have chased after him, but Deke *was* there, so Austin escaped around the end of the high fence bordering the parking lot, leaving Kristen feeling on the edge of nausea. She had to tell her family before he did.

"Saw you on the cameras," Deke said, jarring her back to the here and now. "Thought the guy might be giving you grief, but I guess you know him. Everything okay?"

"Yeah. Fine," she said automatically.

Deke frowned down at her, his expression stern. "You better get yourself home."

"I will."

Deke waited until she was safely in her roommate's car before heading back into the casino. Kristen waited until the door shut behind him before she closed her eyes and leaned her forehead onto the steering wheel, acid churning in her stomach. The past two months had taught her about the futility of dying a thousand deaths, worrying about what *might* happen. The problem in this case, was she was certain it *would* happen.

Right or wrong, Austin had an ax to grind and he would rat her out because he could. Most-Likely-to-Succeed Kristen would soon be known as Lied-to-Save-Her-Pride Kristen. And not a white lie. This was a huge lie of omission.

She should have told her family she'd been laid off immediately after it had happened, but her dad had broken his leg in a nasty fall only a few days prior and, on top of that, she hadn't wanted to disappoint her parents...to confess to them that their little overachiever had crashed and burned professionally.

It was stupid, looking back, but she'd been blindsided by her termination and her first instinct had been to hole up, lick her wounds, then find a new job and confess to her family *after* she turned a difficult situation around. The only problem was the "new job" part...and time's nasty habit of slipping by too quickly. But her family had been focused on her father's recovery, so it had been easy to keep the truth quiet while she forged ahead with her half-baked scheme. Easy and stupid and out of character.

Now Austin knew the truth.

Her stomach churned.

She started the small car, settled her hands on the steering wheel, then sat staring at the brick casino wall as the engine idled. She had to tell her family, and she had to do it soon.

Before Austin beat her to the punch.

Chapter Two

L IKE VEGAS, RENO was a city that never slept, but the sidewalks were relatively empty as Austin passed under the Biggest Little City in the World archway. Empty enough that he noticed the car slowing behind him. The traffic light ahead of him was green. No reason to slow, unless…

He shot a quick look over his shoulder. A Ford Escort came to a stop and the driver leaned over to look at him through the tinted passenger window. Austin shoved his hands deeper into his jacket pocket and kept walking. The window whirred down.

"Austin."

Did he really want to continue this?

"Austin…please…"

He rolled his eyes skyward, then reversed course. Stepping over to the car, he braced a hand on the edge of the doorframe as he leaned down to look through the open window. "Do we know each other?"

Kristen's mouth tightened. "Yes." He said nothing and her expression faltered. "Would you get in the car?"

He wasn't certain if it was curiosity or the uncharacteristic note of desperation in her voice that made him reach for the door handle, open the door and settle into the cramped seat. Once he was inside, Kristen focused on the green light beckoning her to move forward, presenting him with a stiff profile.

"Where are you staying?" she asked.

"The Legacy." Only a few blocks away.

"Maybe we can circle the block a few times." Her knuckles were going white on the steering wheel.

He gave a careless shrug. "Circle away, Kris."

She put the car into gear, moving back out onto the street. "I pretended I didn't know you because my family is unaware that I've encountered a few roadblocks."

She sounded like she was reading from cue cards.

"You might work on your inflection, so that you sound more genuine."

She shot him a look. "I am being genuine." She jerked her gaze forward again.

"No, you're being curt and impersonal."

She was also desperate—that was more than obvious. Something was wrong in Kristen Alexander's life and, even as he tried to tamp it down, his protective instinct rose. He tamped harder. "Roadblocks. That's why you're slinging drinks?"

She nodded, and then, instead of circling the block, she pulled into an empty parking spot a couple of blocks past the Legacy. Austin was relieved she was no longer trying to drive—her mind was obviously not on the road.

"Why be ashamed of moonlighting?" He knew the answer. People like Kristen didn't dress up in costumes—especially a costume like this. His gaze slid from the bejeweled feather thing in her hair to the cardigan sweater she wore over the satin corset that barely contained her breasts, down to the super short skirt. Not Kristen's normal style, unless she'd changed one hell of a lot since high school.

Her chin lifted. "I'm not ashamed." The words came out a little too casually. "I just…I didn't want Whit and my folks to worry about me."

It was a legitimate concern. Reno wasn't an easy town in many regards, but his gut told him it wasn't the entire truth.

"I'm asking you not to tell them, Austin."

He cocked his head. Studied her as the traffic light a few yards away turned first yellow, then red. He didn't know her that well. He'd fancied himself wildly in love with her once upon a time, only to discover that having a crush didn't mean you knew someone. Or that they wouldn't humiliate you in public.

When he didn't answer immediately, she swallowed nervously, but kept her gaze glued to the street in front of her. "Allow me to keep my private life private."

"From your sister?"

"Yes."

"Who can finish sentences for you?"

Her jaw muscles tightened. "I told you—I don't want

my family to be nervous on my account."

"They seem to be okay with Whitney's lifestyle." Her sister tended bar in Marietta and wasn't shy about having a good time.

"That's Marietta, and that's Whitney."

Good point. Marietta was a small, warm place compared to the Biggest Little City and Kristen was book smart rather than street smart. "What kind of roadblocks have you run into?"

"That's not the issue."

"Yeah. I think it is." He caught the flash of something that looked a lot like annoyance in her eyes—there then gone—and wondered if it was because he'd dared to question her. "Maybe I'm worried about your wellbeing," he said softly.

Her lips parted and, heaven help him, he couldn't help but notice how sexy her mouth was. Soft pouty lips that promised…well…many things. "You're telling me that you came back to the casino because you were concerned about my wellbeing—not because you wanted to catch me in a lie?"

"The lie was a big part of it." He let out a soft snort. "I mean, come on, Kristen. That is *not* a normal thing to do."

"It is if you're desperate." Kristen closed her mouth, hard, giving Austin the impression that the words had slipped out before she could stop them. It was a good bet that was exactly what had happened.

"Do you want help?" The words came out automatically,

and even though he cursed himself for saying them, knowing full well she'd throw them back at him, he couldn't help making the offer.

Kristen dropped her gaze to her lap, her lush mouth tightening as she battled it out in her head. She finally drew in a deep breath, as if steeling herself, then brought her chin up and leveled a long look at him. "The way you can help most is to not cause my family worry. Don't get revenge on me in this way."

That pissed him off—especially after he'd offered to help. "This isn't about revenge, Kristen."

She didn't look as if she believed him, but she let it go without an argument. "Then please just let things be."

"I'm not promising anything one way or the other." He had a feeling that Whitney would want to know that her sister's life wasn't all roses, and this situation was strange enough that he was going to mull it over before making any promises. But the fact that she assumed he'd tell might get her to do the right thing. Soon. "I'll give you a couple days. That's all I'll promise." He reached for the handle and shoved the door open.

"Austin…"

"A couple of days." He shut the door, then leaned down to give Kristen one last look through the open window. "Have a good life, Kris. I hope it gets better."

AUSTIN STALKED TOWARD the entrance of the Legacy, moving with an unconscious grace despite being angry and favoring his right leg. And to think he'd once been fodder for her fantasies. Kristen popped a fist onto the steering wheel, then jumped when the horn sounded. Austin looked back, but she refused to make eye contact as she put the car in gear and pulled away from the curb.

Some nights were better than others.

This night was a crapfest.

What the hell was she going to do now?

Tell the family. What else?

Her temples started throbbing as she stopped at a light. Her dad would understand—eventually, although it wouldn't be pretty in the beginning—because he was also a driven overachiever. But her mom…her mom was *not* going to understand. The Alexanders had raised their girls to do the right thing. Kristen had failed them, which made her feel sick inside.

She drove home on autopilot, glad to see that the spot where her roommate's boyfriend parked was empty…although at least this boyfriend wore clothes. Nothing started the old blood pumping like stepping out of the bedroom in the wee hours and being confronted by a naked guy.

Except for a confrontation with Austin Harding.

That had got her blood pumping, and it was the reason she wouldn't be sleeping tonight.

Would he tell Whitney?

He might—in a couple of days. She had that. She fully believed he would give her the promised time because, unless he'd changed a lot, that was the kind of guy Austin was. He had a code.

Kristen let herself into the apartment and locked the door before dropping her tote bag on the sofa. The situation would not get better on its own. She had to reconcile her lie. Now. Before it got worse. She'd call home. Confess. As she should have done when she'd first gotten laid off.

Whitney was going to hate her. She'd never kept anything from her twin, except this, and Whitney wasn't going to be sympathetic to the didn't-want-to-stress-the-family argument.

Kristen went into the kitchen and poured a glass of water, then went back to the sofa and sat in the semi-darkness. Her feet hurt. Her head hurt. Her life was spiraling out of her control.

What were the chances of running into a hometown guy in a city this size? And, if she *had* to run into someone, why did it have to be Austin, the only guy she'd ever yelled at in public? A guy who wasn't exactly blameless in what had gone between them many years ago?

Yes, she'd taken a strip off him in public, but he'd started things. Insulted her. And regardless of what people say, an insult in high school, especially from a guy one was secretly infatuated with…although, in her defense, it was hard to find a girl in that school who wasn't infatuated with Austin...*did* feel like the end of the world. Whitney would have shrugged off the insult, flung a few back. Kristen had felt like climbing into a hole. But she hadn't. Not when he'd drawn the line. And she was still kind of proud of herself for that, even if it might bite her in the butt now.

No. Austin was not blameless. Unfortunately, he'd been in the power position a few hours ago, so she couldn't point that out.

Maybe, after she confessed to her family, they could have a word.

The idea made her smile grimly.

She set the water on the end table and pulled her phone out of her bag and typed in Austin's name. American Extreme Bull Riders Tour popped up. Kristen frowned as she studied the lineup of extremely hot guys.

Well, that explained why he was in town. He was a professional bull rider.

He was also pretty damned successful.

She flipped through his internet fan pages, read a few paragraphs of a National Public Radio transcript—Austin on NPR...go figure—then set down the phone. He was successful and articulate. Great. All the better to rat her out.

How had she not known he'd made something of himself?

But then again, *why* would she know? She rarely made it home, due to college and work, and when she had gone home, she'd focused on family or vegged out in the house she and her sister had inherited from their grandmother. Relished the freedom to do nothing—until nothing started to get to her. That was when she and her mom and Whit would tackle one of the many house projects her mom saved for "the girls"—repainting rooms, sorting through the basement, organizing the garage. They always made a trip to the Marvell Ranch, if the roads were clear, and she'd reconnect with her cousins. She always enjoyed that because, even though she and her cousins rarely saw one another anymore, it never felt awkward when they got together again.

Kristen picked the phone back up and scrolled through more screens, stopping at the American Extreme Bull Riders Tour schedule. Her forehead wrinkled as she studied the dates and cities. Brutal. Austin was in a different city every week from January to October. Before Reno, he'd been in California, and before that New Mexico. Next week he'd be in Salt Lake City. That spoke of dedication. Commitment. The things she'd once told him he lacked. The irony of his success and her lack of it was not lost on her.

Her thumb hovered for a moment, then she hit the 'image' button and was rewarded with pages of photos. Austin with his shirt half buttoned. Austin without his shirt. Austin hanging in midair over the back of a bull. Austin throwing his hat.

Austin looking hot as hell.

Kristen clicked out of the screen and set the phone aside.

Enough Austin. The guy could put a wrinkle in her life, and the last thing she should be doing was ogling his semi-naked and very hard body.

AUSTIN JAMMED THE keycard in the lock upside down not once, but twice. Finally, he got the damned thing flipped around and opened the door. The drink he'd had before riding the elevator up to fifteenth floor hadn't kept him from mulling over the situation with Kristen Alexander, but it had affected his motor skills.

He dropped his wallet and change onto the dresser, then went to the window and stared out over the city lights. She'd actually pretended to be someone else to keep her family from knowing that she'd 'hit a few roadblocks'.

That was not normal.

None of your business.

Right.

He'd been told to butt out and he probably would. *Probably.*

Whitney would want to know what was up with her twin. That was a given. The question was, should he tell her? Was it his place to tell her? He and Whit were pretty good friends and had been for years. He liked her, felt easy around her—which was the opposite of how he felt around Kristen. Even in the short amount of time they'd been together tonight, she'd managed to put him on edge, both mentally and physically. Made him aware of how ridiculous his idea of 'melting the ice princess' had been back in the day.

Austin put a hand to his forehead and squeezed. He'd actually said that to his friends. Melt the ice princess. Of course, he'd been two or three beers in at the time, sitting next to a campfire with four of his buddies, discussing rodeo, life and women.

Who you asking to prom?

Kristen Alexander.

No shit? No way!

Yep…I'm going to melt that ice princess.

He unsnapped his shirt, tossed it onto a chair. Wild laughter had ensued. Followed by a few casual bets. His answer had been born of sheer impulse. Kristen Alexander did not run with his crowd, the rodeo crowd. She was on the fast track to success with a full-ride scholarship already in the bag, and she dated only the class elite. Her own kind.

But Austin always had liked setting his sights high, aiming for the impossible. He'd also had three classes with her that year and, sometimes, when she was concentrating and her features relaxed, she looked different. Softer. More approachable. As if the whole perfection thing was an act and there was another person behind the cool exterior, a person more like her carefree sister. He wanted to meet that person.

A few times he'd gotten a glimpse of her, the other Kristen, the one who didn't look so high and mighty. He'd seen her laughing in the corner of the library with her friends on one of his rare visits, and after the librarian had shushed them, they'd looked at one another and then Kristen had burst into laughter. She unsuccessfully tried to turn it into a cough, which only made everyone laugh harder. He'd never seen her laugh before. It had intrigued him.

Not long after that, she'd dropped her books in the middle of the hall a few minutes before the bell when the halls were nearly empty. A flurry of papers had scattered across the tiled floor—more paper than he'd probably produced in all his high school English classes. He'd stopped to help and could still remember how she'd looked up as he knelt next to her, a startled expression chasing across her face before she'd smiled. A tentative, self-conscious smile that had transformed her face as her cheeks went pink.

And then her friends had swooped out of a nearby classroom to save the day, and she'd avoided his gaze as she'd stuffed the papers into her binder. He'd left, but couldn't stop thinking about Kristen Alexander and how she'd seemed more shy than snooty for those few seconds. He'd always found her sexy in a hands-off kind of way, with her full mouth, long legs, firm ass. And now it looked as if there was more to Kristen than she let on. Catnip to a guy who liked a challenge, so he'd set about trying to charm her.

His friends followed his progress closely, since a lot of them had money riding on the deal. Of course, word had gotten to Kristen about his plan to ask her to prom, and she'd sent a short sweet message back to him.

Tell him I don't date losers.

He could still recall the jaw-dropping moment when one of his rodeo buddies passed the message along with a hearty laugh and a slug in the shoulder. "She thinks you're a loser, dude."

Maybe it was because of his father, who'd agonized about feeling like a loser after giving up a promising rodeo career to tend a farm that had gone bankrupt. Or maybe it was the fact that everyone and their grandmother had heard her comeback before he had, and started razzing him about it, but Austin had come close to tipping over after getting the message.

Then he wondered if it was possible to convince her that whatever she'd heard had been taken out of context. Most likely it hadn't, but he had to do what he could.

With damage control in mind, he'd found her at her locker, wrestling a heavy book off the top shelf. She'd looked over her shoulder at him and froze, eyes wide, lips parted. Classic deer in the headlights.

"Austin."

He'd reached out to take the book off the shelf and hand it to her. "I heard you called me a loser." He spoke easily, as if it was no big deal and he was giving her a chance to explain, but people passing by in the hall started to slow their steps. Some came to a standstill. Fine. If she'd called him a loser because of his melt-the-ice-princess remark, then he'd apologize in front of witnesses. Make it right.

Kristen shot a look at the growing crowd and then tilted her chin up. Pressed her full lips tightly together. Refused to answer.

"*Did* you call me a loser?" Austin asked again. "Because if you did, you should own up to it."

Her face had gone totally red. "I did." The quiet words seemed to ring through the hallway.

"Why?" A clear opening for her to mention his campfire boast, and thus a chance for him to apologize and maybe even salvage this situation. She didn't answer immediately, so he'd asked again. "Why?"

She glanced at the crowd as if looking for a means of escape. There wasn't one, so she'd swallowed dryly, then tilted up her chin and said defiantly, "Because you act like one."

The words had felt like ice water hitting him in the face. "What?"

"You don't go to class, you drink too much, you have no goals. You're wasting time when you could be achieving something. You swagger around like you own the school, but you don't respect what goes on here. You *act* like a loser."

Austin had stared at her, stunned. Kristen, who never talked, was talking now, and he didn't like what she had to say.

"I'm not a loser." The words had come gritting out from between his teeth. He was a high school rodeo champion, for fuck's sake, but apparently that didn't count.

She'd hadn't said another word; in fact, she'd looked as if she wanted to melt into the floor, then she'd pressed the book he'd handed to her against her chest, slammed her locker and pushed her way into the crowd, which parted to let her through.

He could still recall the heat in his face as he fought to look as if it were her loss, then turned without a word and walked in the opposite direction, shoulders square, back straight.

But inwardly he was shaken.

All this time he'd been trying to charm his way into her good graces, and she'd thought he was a loser. Shit. Who else thought that? And if they hadn't, did they now?

Austin had never thought of himself as having a fragile ego, but he had been damned glad that graduation was only a month away, because that confrontation had changed the way he felt about himself, school. Kristen.

And his buddies, being the kind of guys they were, didn't let him forget that Kristen Alexander had called him out for being a loser. In their defense, they'd had no idea that he hadn't shaken off the incident—or that her remarks had cut deeply, making him wonder if he really was a loser. He didn't have goals, other than graduation and rodeos, certainly had no long-term plan for the future. That had seemed pretty loser-like.

The craziest part of the situation was that the confrontation had led to him becoming friends with Kristen's twin,

Whitney, who'd looked him up the day after the confrontation. She'd made no excuses for her sister; had simply wanted to check on him. And eventually, after most of their graduating class left Marietta, moving on to better and brighter things, they'd become friends.

Austin turned away from the window and sat on the bed, where he pulled off his new boots: first one, then the other, letting them fall to the floor. The ice packs he'd jammed into the small fridge were cold and he slapped one on his shoulder and another on his hip before reaching for the remote.

Big event tomorrow. It was time for a win. He'd made decent money on the tour thus far, and had avoided serious injury; for the most part, he'd only aggravated old injuries and that he could live with, especially with four long months stretching ahead of him. But he hadn't won yet.

Kristen wouldn't be there to see it, but he was going to show the world what a winner looked like.

Chapter Three

KRISTEN DECIDED TO wait until Sunday to call her parents, a time when her dad wasn't on shift at the hospital and her mother wasn't busy with her many volunteer projects. That way she could talk to them together. Of course, she would call Whitney first—test the waters. Endure twin wrath, because Whit was not going to be happy.

She woke up feeling edgy and out of sorts, but told herself she'd feel better once this was all behind her. She was not a secret keeper. Should have never tried. Now she would be free of her secret, so maybe meeting Austin in the Silver Bow hadn't been the worst thing in the world.

No. It had been.

She could have gone a long time without facing off with the man, and damn him for still being sexy. Kristen was certain that she'd dreamed about him that night, though she couldn't remember anything specific. It wasn't the first time that had happened. Austin had haunted her dreams and her fantasy life during high school, leaving her feeling frustrated and confused. Irritated with herself.

She'd had big plans, which meant she had no business

being attracted to a guy with no goals. A guy who didn't care about his future enough to regularly attend classes. A charismatic risk taker who didn't follow strict plans or fit into a neat box—both of which characterized her life. Strict plans. Neat boxes.

But what if he changed? What if he became more serious? Noticed her? Liked her?

Changed for *her*.

Her knack for mathematics told her that the odds were not in her favor, even if he had talked to her a time or two, and helped her with spilled papers in the hall. After the paper incident, her Austin awareness had intensified, as had the guilt for being attracted to him in the first place. He was not her type, didn't fit into her world...but she couldn't stop thinking about him.

The push and pull continued throughout their senior year, right up until one of her friends had announced that Austin had called her an ice princess—he was asking her to prom to see if he could melt her.

Melt her.

There was no mistaking what her friends thought "melting" entailed, and she'd been beyond embarrassed thinking about Austin laughing about her with his friends. Had he figured out that he was the object of her fantasies? Was he ridiculing her?

In the face of that horror, Kristen had done the only thing she could and sent her message via the Marietta School grapevine, which had done its work in its usual efficient fashion. Austin was a loser and she wanted nothing to do with him. Thus, the face-off and thus the most mortifying moment of her life.

Thank you, Austin.

Five hours later, Kristen parked her roommate's car in her usual spot and headed for the rear entrance of the casino, where she and Austin had their uncomfortable confrontation the night before. Her first indication that something was wrong was when Deke glanced down instead of making eye contact as she walked past his office on her way to punch in. The second was when Hanna, her manager, came into the staff room and told her not to bother changing from her flats into her torturous bootie shoes.

Kristen blinked at her. "Is there a problem?"

Hanna gave a slow nod. "This isn't working, Kristen." There was no note of apology in her voice. She was stating a fact.

"I don't understand." She was only six days into her pro-bationary two weeks.

"When there's an issue with a customer, your options are to either see me to resolve it, or to muscle through. That is a non-negotiable. Yesterday, you did neither. You ignored the table until they left, which tells me that you either don't understand, or don't care about, customer protocol and the reputation of the Silver Bow Casino."

"It was one incident."

Hanna's mouth tightened. "It's more than that. You aren't comfortable with the customers, Kristen. It shows."

"I'm polite with all the customers."

"You're distant. You don't smile." Hanna spoke as if that were a major crime.

Maybe she didn't smile as much as she should, but she wasn't unpleasant. She was trying to smile. "I'll improve if you give me another chance." She'd smile her butt off, even at the people who said rude things to her if it kept a paycheck coming in.

Hanna gave her a weary look. "I don't see this getting better, and it's not fair to the rest of the staff to keep you on the off chance it will. I need to hire someone suited to the position sooner rather than later. HR has already been informed and will mail you your final check."

She hadn't even gotten a first check.

"Hanna…"

"I'm sorry, Kristen. Gather your things. Deke will make certain you get out of the building okay." As if leaving the building okay was an issue. He was going to make certain she left without making a scene.

Feeling numb, Kristen shouldered her tote bag and followed Hanna out of the staff room. Deke was waiting at the hallway leading to the parking lot entrance, hands on his utility belt.

"You're lucky," he said in a low voice as she passed in front of him. "The last girl they let go, they did it at the end of her shift."

"At least she got the shift." Kristen's stomach was so tight she thought she was going to puke.

"This isn't the right job for you."

"Obviously." But it had been a job.

As she pushed her way out through the exit, she barely held back the tears. She was a flat-out failure. More than that, she was a double failure.

The heavy metal door shut behind her and there she was. Alone in a parking lot. No job. No future. She closed her eyes, pulled in a long breath. Her tote bag felt heavy on her shoulder. Hell, the world felt heavy on her shoulders.

She didn't know what to do. Her reserves were shot. Her savings were low. Her grapevine was dried and withered. She'd pulled in what had seemed like her last favor to get this job and now she had no job.

Was she going to have to go home and sponge off her family until she got back on her feet? That hurt. A lot.

And she'd have to ship her stuff home—not that she had a lot that wasn't in storage, but there was more than she could fit into a couple of suitcases. Maybe she could rent a truck.

A quick internet search after she'd gotten into her borrowed car told her no, she would not be doing that.

Not without calling Whitney and asking for a loan. And explaining why she needed it. That would be a painful talk. Things had been stilted between them the last couple of times they'd spoken. Her sister knew that something was off, but Kristen had stonewalled. Told her everything was fine. She'd been over three weeks into unemployment at that point and certain she'd land a new job soon.

Yeah. That had really worked out.

As soon as she got home, Kristen called her sister. Confessed everything. Whitney did not take the news well.

"Now wait…one more time. You've been out of work for *how long*?"

Kristen pressed her palm to her forehead. The call was as painful as she'd predicted—maybe more so—because her sister was just this side of livid. She'd explained about taking an interim job, and about how she'd run into Austin, but Whitney was bypassing all that and latching on to the fact that her closest relative in the world hadn't poured out her troubles as she'd gone through them.

"Whit…you guys were dealing with Dad's accident and I thought I was going to land a job in no time."

"And when that didn't happen? When Dad got better and the weeks stretched on?"

"It felt like it was too late to confess."

"Why?"

"Because I'd lied by omission for too long," Kristen blurted. "Surely you can understand that?"

"No. I don't think that I can. It's…unacceptable." Whitney let out an audible sigh. "*I* would have told *you*!"

"You don't know that." Because a year ago, Kristen never

would have seen herself doing what she'd done.

"Yeah. I do. Because you're my sister and I'd damned well be asking you for help if I got into a bind."

"You know that for sure?"

"I do."

They could argue about what Whitney may or may not have done all day, so Kristen pushed on to her main source of worry. "I don't know how to tell Mom."

"Well, you'd better think of something." The words practically spit sparks.

"Whitney—"

"I can't help it. I'm *pissed.*"

"I'm coming home." She had to talk to her mom face to face and, like it or not, she needed sanctuary. She needed the safety of home.

"You do that. I'll lie to Mom until you get here."

"Damn it, Whit—"

"No. You don't get a 'damn it'. And you don't get to be angry. You get to eat humble pie and get your ass home."

Now Kristen sighed. "I will."

"Let me know when you leave…and how you're traveling. I want dates and times."

Those were orders. "Yes." Whit still felt protective, but she wasn't going to make things easier for her. Not until she cooled down anyway. That worked, because Kristen didn't want things easy. She felt like crap and she needed to pay some penance.

The connection ended and Kristen found herself holding a dead phone to her ear.

One enraged sister to deal with when she got home. To be followed by trusting parents, who would be no happier to have been kept in the dark than Whit had been.

It's your life. You're an adult.

True, but she hadn't acted like one. Now she needed to go home, do damage control. Get her life back on track...somehow.

The bus schedule was a nightmare. The ticket cost close to two hundred dollars, which she didn't have because the Silver Bow hadn't paid her yet, and the trip took forty-three hours. She could get as far as Butte in twenty-three hours, and then she had to wait twenty hours to transfer to another bus for the three-hour trip to Marietta.

That made a hell of a lot of sense.

Who did she know in Butte who might give her a ride to Marietta? She'd lost contact with her old friends during the years she'd been to college and started her job. Most of her closest friends were off conquering worlds in far-flung cities. And they probably still had jobs.

"I tallied it up." Her roommate, Lynn, came out of her bedroom and set a paper on the table. "I'm sorry you're paying for next month's rent, but it's too late to get someone else and you know I can't swing this alone."

Kristen didn't expect her to.

"That's okay. I need a place to keep my stuff until I

make arrangements to take it…somewhere." Presumably back home.

"I'll prorate the rent if things move faster." Lynn was trying hard to help and Kristen appreciated the feeling of support.

Kristen worked up a smile. "You've been great. I wouldn't have been able to work for *six* whole days if you hadn't lent me your car."

Lynn smiled back and reached out to touch Kristen's arm, which brought her close to breaking point. She was going home with her tail between her legs, to make peace with her sister and to confess to her parents. The winner was going home a loser. She'd made one poor decision after another after being laid off and it had all caught up with her.

"How did things go with your sister?"

"Not good. And I can't blame her. I broke trust. Now I need to smooth the waters. In person."

"You're going home *now*?"

"I…think I'd better. For the sake of family relations." And her finances. She couldn't keep living in the city.

"If you can't make it back before the end of May, Jason and I will pack up for you. Take your stuff to storage."

"I'll make it back." She had almost forty days to figure out what to do with the storage warehouse full of the furniture she'd bought during what she now thought of as 'the good times'—the time when she was employed. She could probably borrow a truck and trailer from her Marvell cousins

JEANNIE WATT

and put things in storage on their ranch. Or she could sell it, but that would take time.

Lynn took a seat on the other side of the table, moving aside the vase of colored daisies to make room for her elbows. The flowers, coupled with the golden glow of the setting sun slanting in through the blinds, made the apartment feel warm and cheery—the antithesis of Kristen's life. "How are you getting home?" Lynn asked.

"The bus." She explained the trip without mentioning the part where she was going to use the last of her available cash for the ticket, focusing instead on the ridiculous twenty-hour layover, which she'd probably end up enduring, to pay penance, if nothing else.

"Your sister won't pick you up?"

"I'm, uh, kind of afraid to ask."

"And there's no other way?"

There was probably a way. There was always a way, if one looked hard enough. Someone who could help without being put out.

Someone who could help.

Austin.

Bad idea. *Very* bad idea.

He'd offered to help… Had he meant it?

Even if he had, she'd tossed his offer right back at him. Would he want to help now?

Would it hurt to ask?

According to the American Extreme Bull Riders schedule, he was going to Salt Lake City for his next tour stop. Maybe…

Kristen pulled out her phone and pulled up a search engine. There was a small touring bus line that ran a route from SLC to Livingston, passing through Marietta on its way. It was called Montana…something.

Montana Vista Tour Line.

And the ticket was a quarter of the cost of the other ticket. Almost affordable.

"Do you have an idea?" Lynn asked.

Kristen looked up from her phone. "I might." What in the world did she have to lose by asking Austin for a lift to Salt Lake? Her pride? She'd dropped that along the wayside when she'd climbed into that saloon girl outfit and pasted a fake smile on her face for money.

And maybe she owed Austin some penance, too.

He probably thought so.

"I ran into a hometown acquaintance at the casino yesterday. He's going to Salt Lake City soon. He might be able to help me out."

"Ask him," Lynn said with an encouraging smile. "What would it hurt?"

"Right. I'll ask him," Kristen said. Why not? All it would take was exactly what her sister had suggested—a huge portion of humble pie.

AUSTIN SMILED AT his last signee, a kid in his early teens, dressed in beat-up cowboy boots and jeans and a brand new American Extreme Bull Riders ball cap. It'd been a busy signing day for his sponsor—a couple of hours at the local Boot Barn that afternoon, and then an hour on the concourse before the big event. Now it was get-into-his-head time.

"Austin."

His back stiffened at the sound of the familiar voice. *Son of a bitch.* Really?

He turned to find Kristen Alexander walking toward him across the concourse, wearing worn jeans and an oversized Nevada Wolf Pack sweatshirt. She slowed as she approached, looking both determined and nervous.

"You want an autograph?" he asked as she came to a stop a few feet away from him.

"I have nothing to sign." She pushed her long reddish-brown hair over her shoulder, looking patently self-conscious. Had she come to apologize? To ask him once again to keep his mouth shut?

"That doesn't slow a lot of women down." He'd been asked to sign some interesting things…and places.

She caught his meaning, tipped up her chin. "Thank you. I don't need an autograph."

He shifted his weight onto his good hip, folded his arms over his chest. Basically took on his in-your-face bull rider stance. "What *do* you need?"

"I need a ride to Salt Lake City."

Not anything close to what he'd been expecting. "Why?"

"I got fired. Again." The words barely made it out of her mouth before she pressed it tightly shut again and swallowed. She was going to cry. If it had been anyone else, he would have been more affected. She blinked a few times and managed to regain her composure. "I need to go home."

"You're asking *me* for a ride?" She had to be borderline desperate.

"To Salt Lake City."

"Then what? Hitchhike?"

"I have enough money to take the Montana Vista Tour bus from Salt Lake to Marietta."

Enough money for a bus? "Fuck, Kristen. Are things that bad?"

"They aren't good." She closed her mouth as a couple of security guards walked by.

He took her by the arm and led her behind a wide concrete column. "Maybe you can give me a little more information."

Kristen glanced down at the floor for a brief moment, then met his gaze dead on. "I lost my job over two months ago. I didn't tell the family because I thought I'd get another fast. I told Whitney this morning. Now I need to tell my mom. I want to do it face to face."

"You weren't moonlighting as a cocktail waitress."

"No." She held his gaze, her expression bordering on defiant as she said, "That was my job—the only one I could get that paid enough to allow me to live and not default on loans. I sold my car, but it was old and I barely got anything for it. Enough for a month's rent and some groceries."

It took him a moment to process all that she'd just confessed.

"I'm asking you for help." Which he'd offered her in a moment of weakness. "And I understand if you don't want to give it."

He leaned his shoulder against the concrete pillar. In a few hours, his name would be called and he'd walk through smoke and fire to his appointed spot and the crowd would cheer, because he did something that most people couldn't do. He faced a ton of raging bovine week after week and came out alive. Surely he could get through this.

"Yeah. I'll take you to Salt Lake. But it won't be a direct trip."

"Meaning?"

"I have a stop along the way." He glanced past her to the center arena where the crews were setting up. "I have to get taped up. We can discuss details later. Are you staying for the performance?"

"I can't afford it. I had to sidestep security to get in to talk to you."

"You…" *Sidestepped security?* "Never mind." He reached into his shirt pocket, pulled out one of the two passes he had for special guests. "Meet me at the north exit door after the event is over."

She gave a short nod. "I will." She cleared her throat. "Thank you. And…I want to apologize for the things I said to you…that day…in high school."

"Did you mean them?"

She pressed her lips together briefly. "I was…wrong."

"Well, I guess life has a way of sorting out the real winners and losers."

He smiled a not very friendly smile, then turned and headed down the concrete steps to the change room.

Chapter Four

ALMOST TWO HOURS after Austin had handed her the pass to the bull-riding event, Kristen was still chewing on his remark about life separating the winners and losers. She'd failed, yes. But failing wasn't the same as being a loser.

You *accused Austin of being a loser.*

It was clear now that he wasn't—he'd simply had a different vision of success. One that differed radically from her own. But…was bull riding a real job? He had money, yes. But did he have stability?

Do you have either of those things?

Kristen was getting tired of being heckled by her own inner voice, so when the house lights dimmed she sat up in her seat and focused on the dark arena. She'd been to a lot of rodeos as a kid and not one of them had started in darkness.

The music began—a deep thrumming that made the floor vibrate beneath her feet—and spotlights swirled over the crowd as the announcer welcomed fans to Reno, Nevada! Flames ignited on either side of the arena, traveling in long straight lines until they branched out and then the letters AEBR burst into flames.

Kristen's mouth dropped open. The Copper Mountain Rodeo in Marietta needed to think about doing this. Very impressive. And even more impressive were the bull riders now striding through the manmade smoke and fire to take their places along the flaming lines. There was something primal about the smoke, the fire, the men about to risk their lives in an attempt to stay on a bull's back for eight long seconds, and, as the music reached a crescendo and the fans cheered, Kristen understood why Austin did this. The feeling of power and anticipation was overwhelming. And the bull riders themselves…these were guys who'd fight wolves and then catch you something to eat for dinner. Alpha guys.

The kind of guys she avoided like the plague because they intimidated her.

But watching them stride out of the arena, walking shoulder to broad shoulder, the long fringe on their chaps flapping with each step…maybe she was succumbing to alpha fever. Temporarily.

As soon as the lights came up, a crew gathered around the far chute. Moments later the gate swung open and a bull exploded out, spinning violently to first the right and then the left as the crowd cheered. The rider released his grip at the horn, did half a flip and landed in a heap in the dirt. A split second later he was on his feet, racing for the rails as two bull fighters distracted the black and white bull.

"T.J. Casey setting the bar on Ignitor, ladies and gentleman. Eighty-nine points!"

Eighty-nine was a decent score. Austin had his work cut out for him.

Kristen sat back in her seat, only to come forward again for the next ride. And the next. The pace and the energy were crazy. A rider named Cody was up and Austin was announced on deck. Kristen realized that her hands were clenched into tight fists and she made an effort to relax.

He was her ride to Salt Lake City, not her husband or boyfriend. But regardless of who he was, she wanted him safe. Wanted all of the guys to be safe. No one had made eight seconds since T.J. Casey had ridden the first bull out and Kristen wondered if any of them would.

The gate opened and the crew fell back as a giant midnight black bull reared out of the chute, throwing his head back and just missing Cody's face. Less than a second later the animal hit the ground with all four feet and then launched himself into an epic series of spins.

The whistle blew and the rider released, kicking a leg over the bull's massive head and landing on both feet. The crowd erupted and Kristen was right there on her feet with them.

Oh yeah, she was definitely coming down with alpha fever.

And hopefully she'd be fully recovered by the time she met Austin at the north door of the venue following the event.

LIFE HAS A way of separating the winners and losers.

True enough, and Austin hoped karma wasn't going to bite him in the ass for pointing that out to Kristen. Hard Landing, his draw for the evening, rolled his eye and flicked an ear as Austin eased into place just in front of the flank strap. He handed the tail of his rope to Gage to hold tight as he worked the rosin in.

"You've got this," Gage muttered.

Austin nodded. He did have it. Once the rosin was warm, he slid his hand into place, finished his wraps and gave his glove a couple pounds. Gage pulled the rope tight and then stepped back as Austin slid forward, almost on top of his hand. The sharp scent of bovine sweat stung his nostrils as he took a deep breath, then nodded. He loved this moment. Lived for this moment, when anything and everything was possible.

The gate opened. Hard Landing reared and then launched into an explosive twisting buck, bringing his ass up over his ears. Austin pushed deep into his feet, held his center as the bull slammed back to earth, then reared again, twisting his body sideways, rolling Austin away from his hand. He corrected before the bull started a series of body-jarring spins. Gritting his teeth, Austin fought gravity and managed to keep from being sucked down into the well before the bull flipped his center of gravity and spun the opposite direction, jerking Austin hard on each jolting landing.

Hard Landing's hooves slammed into the ground, tossing up dirt as he whirled. The horn sounded and Austin released, allowing the bull's momentum to toss him free. He landed, then automatically rolled into a ball as Hard Landing took a pass at him with his blunt-ended horn before the bull fighter intervened.

Having made his point, Hard Landing flicked his tail and trotted to the gate as Austin got to his feet.

"Ninety-four points!"

If he'd had a hat, he would have thrown it in the air. Instead he raised a hand, acknowledged the crowd, then crossed the arena to sit out the next six rides.

No one came close to his score.

Finally. The big win. And it didn't hurt one bit that Kristen Alexander was in the audience when it happened. Vindication was sweet.

After changing, he headed down the long hallway leading to the rear of the facility. Kristen was waiting by the door as planned, staring off in the opposite direction as he approached. When she heard his footsteps, she turned, her face taking on an expression of cool politeness. Emphasis on cool. Hello, Kristen from high school.

"You're here," he said, for lack of anything better to say.

"Yes." She pushed her hands deep into her jacket pockets, tilted the corners of her mouth up into a semi-smile, as if everything was normal between them. Maybe after an eight-hour road trip they would be more normal.

And pigs would fly.

"Congratulations." She sounded like she meant it, so he nodded in acknowledgment before pushing the door open and following her out into the crisp night air.

"Where's your car?"

She pointed to the far end of the lot.

"Let's talk in my truck and then I'll take you to your car."

Under normal circumstances, he might have suggested that she come with him to eat, but these were not normal circumstances. He led the way to his road machine and opened the door for her. Kristen started to get in, but her foot slipped on the running board and he automatically reached out to grab her by the waist before she took a facer.

"I'm okay." She stepped away as if he'd burned her with his touch, then brushed her hands down her sides, wiping away all traces of contact.

Austin frowned at her. Fine. She didn't like to be touched, but it wasn't like he'd grabbed her for any reason other than to save her some bruising. "If you say so."

Halfway pissed, he stalked around the truck, leaving Kristen to climb into the passenger seat on her own. This time she made it in.

"Nice truck," she said as he got into the driver's seat without wincing, even though his hip felt like it was on fire.

He was moving stiffly, but he was moving, and that was a plus.

"Yeah. Fruits of my labor." He fiddled with the keys he'd yet to slide into the ignition, before meeting her gaze. Her cheeks were still flushed and that mouth… He wasn't going to think about her mouth. "I thought we'd better go over my plans for the next few days. If they don't mesh with yours, then you'll need to work out something else."

"What are your plans?" she asked politely.

Cody Galen popped his hand on the hood as he and Gus and Josh ambled by, making Kristen jump. Austin nodded at his teammates, who didn't seem to recognize Kristen as the waitress from the casino, then turned back to Kris. "I'm making a side trip to a friend's ranch. Spring branding. I go every year. They kind of work their schedule around me."

Her eyebrows drew together. "How long is the side trip?"

"A couple days. They brand tomorrow."

"The tour bus to Marietta only runs on Monday, Thursday and Saturday during the off-season."

He shook his head. Not his problem. "So you go home on Thursday."

"I guess so."

He let out a breath after several seconds of silence, balling his fist up on his sore thigh. "If that's not agreeable, then you're going to have to come up with something that doesn't involve me." There was only one option if she was traveling with him, because he wasn't about to change plans.

"It's agreeable." She spoke civilly, but her demeanor was growing more distant by the moment, as if he was somehow in the wrong.

"Why don't you ask Whitney to drive down to pick you up?"

"Long story."

"I have time."

Her eyebrows lifted. "That isn't part of the deal."

There was something in her rapidly cooling attitude that jabbed at him. He wrapped his fingers around the keys, then released his grip so that he was holding them loosely in his palm. "I'll tell you what *is* part of the deal—you don't treat me like dirt and I let you ride in my truck."

Her cheeks went red. "I—" He raised an eyebrow. Waited. Her gaze faltered briefly, then she drew in a breath. "I'm not trying to treat you like dirt."

The words rang true, although the cynical part of him wondered if it was because she really needed the ride. "Then what the hell, Kristen? Why do you do that...cold thing?"

"I'm nervous."

His jaw dropped a little. "What?"

She scowled at him as she met his gaze dead on. "Nervous, Austin. Scared. Not everyone feels comfortable in social situations."

"Get out."

Her eyebrows lifted. "I'm not kidding."

No. She wasn't. "This isn't a social situation. This is you

and me."

She gave him a fierce frown. "I get self-conscious in certain situations, okay? And when I do, I clam up and go all cold and then people think I'm stuck up."

"Wait," he said as the pieces fell into place. "You're saying you're shy?"

"Overachievers can be shy, too. And it's really more a case of social anxiety."

Austin narrowed his eyes as he studied her. Shy? She'd always looked like she had everything figured out.

"This is why you spent most of your time in freeze mode?" The question slipped out without a lot of forethought, but he stood behind it. He honestly wanted to know.

She gave him a sarcastic look. "Kind of fitting for an ice princess, don't you think?"

Nailed. Shit.

"Heard about that, huh?"

She gave a small sniff. "Marietta High School was not a place to keep secrets. Of course, I knew about it. And the bets."

He'd had nothing to do with the bets, but he could see how that would be disturbing. "Before or after you took me down?"

"Before."

"You never said anything…you know…when you yelled at me."

She let out a huff of breath. "You mean like 'How dare you?' That would only have made things worse. It would have appeared that I cared."

"Did you?"

"No."

He didn't believe her. It had been a small incident, years ago. One that he would have filed under "Failed Missions/Lost Bets" if it hadn't been for his shock at being pegged as a loser by a woman who'd not only meant it, but was able to outline the reasoning behind her conclusion as well. In front of his friends, who never forgot anything. It had kind of changed his life...and maybe it had changed hers, too.

"It didn't bother you at all?"

She moistened her lips. "It bothered me."

"I apologize. That was a swaggering teenage boy speaking."

She gave a short nod, not quite looking at him. "Accepted. And I apologize for..." Her voice trailed as she searched for words, so he helped her out.

"Ripping me a new one?"

"Yes."

He pressed his shoulder against the cool glass of the window as he studied her. "Are you going to freeze me out on the drive?"

"I'll try not to."

"If you do, I'll drop you at the nearest truck stop." He

was only half-kidding.

"Noted." She spoke with a straight face, disappointing him in a way, but he was sore and tired and needed to get some sleep. A few hours anyway. Verbal antics could wait. Time to cut to the chase.

"Give me your phone." Kristen handed it over more easily than he'd expected and he entered his number in it, then sent himself a text. His phone chimed and he handed her phone back and put the truck in gear. Her car was one of the few still left in the spectator part of the lot.

"I thought you sold your car?"

"This is my roommate's car."

He stopped close to the little Ford and Kristen opened the door. "Better give me your address."

She rattled it off and he entered it in his map app. "Okay. Tomorrow. Five-thirty sharp. Pack light."

KRISTEN UNLOCKED LYNN'S car and got inside. Once the engine started, Austin pulled out of the lot, but he waited at the four-way stop until she came up behind him. She followed him as far as the Legacy, then continued on to south Reno.

She had her ride to Salt Lake City. Now all she had to do was to pack light and be ready to go at five-thirty, which was about six hours away. Lynn was already in bed when she let herself into the apartment, but her roomie padded out into the living room in bare feet not long after she closed the door. From inside Lynn's room, her boyfriend snored softly.

"Did everything work out?"

Kristen tried to look upbeat as she said, "It did. I have a ride to Salt Lake and I can catch the bus there. He'll pick me up at five-thirty tomorrow."

Lynn brushed back her hair. "Early."

"I know. But…" she gave a small shrug as if traveling with Austin was her preferred method of travel "…he's on a schedule."

"I looked up your bull riding friend while you were gone." She pretended to fan her face. "He's something. In fact, every guy on that tour is something. Kind of makes me want to come along."

"I'd love to have you along." The words were heartfelt. A buffer would be a godsend, but it wasn't going to happen. It would be just her and Austin—and his ranch friends, of course—for the next day or two.

If he could take it, so could she.

She said good night to Lynn and headed to her room, where she pulled out her suitcase and started packing. She hadn't brought a lot to Lynn's place, so it didn't take long to throw clothes she'd need for the trip into the bag. Her work wardrobe hung untouched in the narrow closet and Kristen stood, hands on hips, studying it. Investment pieces. High-end skirts and jackets. Crazy expensive shoes. Dress for the level of employment you want to attain, she'd been taught, so she had.

And gotten laid off.

She stroked the pale gray silk and wool blend blazer hanging in front of her. Her last major splurge/investment. Her mouth flattened for a moment, then she pulled it out of the closet along with the shell pink skirt and white silk top that went with it. Nothing saying she wasn't going to interview in the near future. The firms in Reno might be ignoring her, but that didn't mean there weren't firms in Montana hiring.

She rolled the suit in a dry-cleaning bag and made room for it in her suitcase, along with her Christian Louboutins. With a defiant twist of her lips, she closed the suitcase. She was not going to feel guilty about investment pieces. Poor planning, yes. Shoes that would last forever, no.

Even if she now wished she'd put off buying them until she'd been just a wee bit more secure.

The last thing she dealt with was her Silver Bow 'uniform', the cost of which would be deducted from her first paycheck, leaving her with next to nothing, except for her tips. She wadded it up and stuffed it into a plastic bag. The bootie shoes that killed her feet went in on top. Waste of money, but what could she do? Regrets weren't going to help her move forward.

She tiptoed out of the room and set down her suitcases next to the door and dumped the plastic bag with the costume into the trash. If she went to sleep right now, she'd get close to five hours.

If she went to sleep right now.

Fat chance, that.

KRISTEN KNEW SHE looked like hell when Austin parked in front of her apartment complex early the next morning. She'd tried to brighten her overly pale face with blush, ended up looking like a feverish clown, and scrubbed it off just before he arrived. She didn't need to impress him, or be intimidated by him, so she was annoyed that her heart beat faster as she let herself out of the apartment.

It wasn't the prospect of sparring with Austin for the next few of days that had her feeling edgy—it was the unknowns in her future. She had no job, a big confession to make, a branding with people she didn't know.

Right.

Austin got out of the truck, came around the back and then held out his hand for her suitcase. Kristen scowled at him. He didn't budge and she couldn't place her suitcase into the bed of the truck unless he moved. Apparently, he couldn't help doing the guy thing, so rather than make a point by walking around him, she relinquished the case and he set it in the bed of the truck.

She got into the cab, taking care when she stepped on the

tubular steel running board, and found her safety belt. The truck smelled of leather and oil, rosin and guy. A heady mixture that stirred something in her that she didn't want stirred. Not one little bit. She settled her hands in her lap and stared straight ahead as he put the truck in gear, wondering if this felt as unreal to him as it did to her. And if every muscle in his body was as taut as hers.

Every muscle of his very hard body.

His shirt sleeves were rolled up and the sinews in his bare arms stood out. Judging by what she could see, there wasn't an ounce of fat on the guy. Just solid muscle. There was probably a six-pack under his T-shirt.

Big deal.

Except that he smelled good.

You are in control.

Yeah. Right. Totally in control.

Okay—you can fake being in control.

Exactly.

Austin navigated through town like he lived there, thanks to the phone app that talked him onto the freeway. As they merged with the early morning traffic, heading to I80, which would eventually take them to Salt Lake City, he rolled his shoulders as if taking the kinks out.

"Sore?" She surprised herself by speaking. Surprised him, too, if the look he gave her was anything to judge by.

"I'm pretty much always sore in one way or another."

"I see." Because talking to him made her feel self-conscious, she sounded stiff. Formal. Cold. Exactly the way she didn't want to sound, because she didn't want him to call her on her attitude again.

"You get used to it." He glanced over at her. "Did you much sleep last night?"

She assumed he was commenting on her pale face and tired eyes, but she decided to take the comment at face value. So much easier that way. "Not much. I packed. Then I lay on my bed and stared at the ceiling." She glanced over at him. "How was your evening?"

"I slept." His inflection was dry, but there was no trace of irony in his expression.

"How long to your friend's ranch?"

"Four hours give or take."

She directed her gaze forward, doing her best to ignore him, but that was impossible. It was as if the cab of the truck was growing smaller by the second. She stared out the window, watched the river go by, worried her hands together in her lap, then stopped when she realized what she was doing.

"Is this how the entire trip is going down?" Austin finally asked.

She felt herself start to flush. "I'm not good at small talk." Which should have been obvious to him by now.

"Maybe you should practice." She shot him a startled look and was rewarded with a bland smile. "What could it hurt?"

"If you have to ask, then you don't have a shy bone in your body."

"Don't you mean a socially anxious bone?"

Her mouth tightened briefly. "Yes. That's exactly what I mean."

He gave her a wicked smile. "Guilty." He brought his gaze back to the road, making Kristen feel relatively safe until he said. "Name a topic."

"What?"

"Name. A. Topic."

Kristen gave Austin a pained look. "I apologized. Do you have to torture me, too?"

He gave her another look, but this one wasn't so much wicked as hard. "Yeah. I think I do."

Chapter Five

KRISTEN KEPT HER mouth stubbornly closed as they rounded a series of corners. She probably thought he was making a point about who was in the figurative driver's seat as well as the literal one with his insistence on talking, but he wasn't. There were things he wanted to know. Questions he wanted answered, and he wasn't going to take social anxiety as an excuse.

"Here's a topic," he said, once the road straightened out again. "Did you really think you could get away with pretending not know me at the saloon?" More than that, pretending to be someone else.

Kristen sat straighter in her seat, but didn't attempt to dodge the question, possibly because she sensed what a lost cause that would be. "I'd hoped."

"Did you think I was that stupid?"

"I was banking on drunk, actually. And pretending not to know you seemed so outrageous, I thought I might get away with it."

"You didn't get away with it."

"You weren't drunk." She smoothed the hem of the

flowery shirt she wore.

"The situation bothered me."

"Enough that you came back to the casino. I noticed."

"I don't like being lied to."

"I don't like being ratted out." Kristen started pleating the fabric of her shirt between her fingers again, then stopped. "Would you have told my sister?"

"Maybe. What you did was kind of crazy." He glanced her way. "But I wouldn't have told her out of revenge." It still ticked him off that she thought he operated that way.

"Did you *ever* think of revenge?" she asked.

"No." His fingers tightened on the wheel as he thought back on his reaction to their public face-off. "But I did kind of hate you for a while. You shocked the hell out of me. I thought I was a prize until then." True story. He'd been good at bronc riding—not as good as his brother, but he was close. And the girls seemed to find him attractive. All but one.

"Guys who are prizes go to class."

He frowned at her. For an alleged shy girl, she was holding her own. He'd expected her to try to clam up. "Do you have a guy in your life?"

Her chin lifted ever so slightly. "I do not."

"Have you ever?" He was curious as to whether anyone had managed to battle through her defenses. If there were guys out there, unlike him, who recognized the difference between what she called social anxiety and arrogance. He still wasn't totally clear on what the difference was because the result seemed to be the same. People got put off.

"None of your business."

And there's a limit. "Fair enough."

There was a note of challenge in her voice as she asked, "How about you? Women?"

"I'm not shy."

"Well, bully for you." The telltale color was once again staining her cheeks, giving her a vulnerable look that belied the cool note in her voice. This was the high school Kristen he'd caught intriguing glimpses of. A touch vulnerable. A touch uncertain. After she'd taken him down, he'd decided he'd been imagining things. Maybe not.

"Actually, there is no woman in the picture."

"It doesn't matter."

"Then why did you ask?"

"Because you did." She turned her attention to the side window as they emerged from the canyon, watching the scenery with such intense focus that she had to be developing a crick in her neck. She was shutting down, drawing into herself.

Not going to happen.

He waited until they passed the town of Fernley before asking, "Why did you get fired from the casino?"

Kristen let out a soft snort. "You have no mercy, do you?"

"Not much."

She turned her gaze toward him and calmly replied, "I got fired from the casino because I shirked my duty with your table because I was afraid to come back *and* because I didn't smile."

He shot her a frowning look. "You're kidding."

"Nope. I was polite, but apparently too distant with the customers." Kristen pushed her hair back from her face with both hands. "Ice princess, remember?" Austin lifted his eyebrows, surprised at the reference, but before he could speak, she said, "It's hard to break a lifelong habit."

"You're trying?"

She nodded. "In college, I discovered that people avoided me because they thought I was judging them. I'm trying to be friendlier."

"How's that working out for you?" Because in his view, she had a ways to go, although being aware of the problem was a big step forward.

"I got fired from the casino. Remember?" She gave him a look. "Maybe we can talk about you for a while."

"I'm an open book." He slowed as he spotted a highway patrol vehicle parked in the median, then sped up once he was around the corner. "Nothing about me that you can't find on a fan site or Wikipedia."

"Does that mean we're done with small talk? I can just silently research you on my phone?"

"We're talking to ease the tension." Halfway true. Kristen was still tense, but in a different way than before.

"What tension?"

He met her wide green eyes. "Tell me you didn't just say that."

"I said it."

He reached out and lightly touched her hand, which was resting on the console. She jerked it into her lap. "*That* tension. It's not healthy to be that wound up all the time."

Her eyes flashed. "I appreciate the ride, but enough, okay?"

She was serious and he felt a twinge of regret for pushing to get a reaction from her. "All right."

"You make me jumpy, Austin."

It always surprised him when she was candid. "Because you're shy?"

"Because you're *you*."

He didn't know how to take that and the closed-off expression on her face wasn't giving him any clues. "I apologize for touching you."

She let out a breath and once again stopped her fingers from working the edge of her flowy shirt. "Don't."

"Why not?" he asked on a note of surprise.

Her jaw set before she said, "Because I don't hate it. I just…don't know how to handle it."

Austin gave his head a small, bemused shake. "I'll watch myself."

"Thank you." With that she turned to stare at the passing scenery, shutting him out once and for all.

Austin let her be.

KRISTEN HAD FULLY intended to control the situation—and her mouth—as they drove to Salt Lake City. Unfortunately, Austin had a way of short-circuiting her strategies. How was it that she'd said things to him that she'd never said to anyone else? Not even her sister?

She'd spoken the truth about not hating it when he touched her—and not knowing how to handle it. And these were just small innocent touches. What would it be like if he really touched her?

She shifted her gaze sideways, watched his profile as he drove. He was a million miles away. Thinking about bulls? Or the road? Or maybe her?

She didn't know. Wouldn't know. She pulled out her phone, went to the news app and started to read. It wasn't until they pulled into the Callahan Ranch that service faltered. She set her phone aside and Austin finally spoke. "If at all possible, be nice to my friends."

Her eyes widened, but he simply stared at her, showing no sign of remorse for his bald statement. Which made her wonder just how much of a bitch he thought she was.

"What I'm saying is don't take out your feelings about me on them."

"No worries," she replied coolly as she reached for her

door handle.

Half a dozen trucks were parked near the barn and a group of five or six people were gathered near the chutes.

"Austin!" A small woman with a thick blonde braid, dressed in jeans, a flannel shirt and a canvas vest, started toward him, clipboard in hand.

"Ellie." Austin caught her in a tight embrace, lifting her feet off the ground.

Kristen folded her arms over her middle, staying rooted next to the front bumper of the truck and feeling awkward. Nothing new there.

"Unhand my bride," a tall dark-haired man demanded as he broke away from the group. He also pulled Austin into a hug, only he lifted Austin off his feet.

"Easy," Austin said on a choked laugh. "Hard Landing gave me a hard landing last night."

"But you won! Congratulations." Ellie gave him another hug before looking over at Kristen. "And you brought a friend."

"I did. Kristen and I went to high school together. We bumped into each other in Reno, and I'm giving her a ride home."

More like halfway home. Kristen worked up a smile, feeling very much as she had in the Silver Bow, and came forward. Austin introduced her to Ellie and Clinton Callahan, as well as to Katherine, Ellie's aunt, and the rest of the branding crew—Tom, Clay and Rusty—all of whom seemed to know Austin well. She was the odd man out.

Nothing new there.

"Would you mind manning the clipboard?" Ellie asked. "We're one hand short, so I'm delighted that you came."

"Sure. Just tell me what to do."

A shadow crossed the woman's face. "Have you ever been to a branding?"

"A few," she said dryly. "My mom grew up on a ranch in Montana. We branded twice a year."

Ellie's eyebrows lifted in surprise, probably because Kristen was dressed in clothing no one wore to a branding— running shoes, skinny jeans and a flowered tunic top—and then she smiled. "Excellent." She gave Austin a thumbs-up. "Nice work, Austin. Better than last time…"

He smiled sheepishly, then went to join the men who were heading into the pen where the calves were being held, making Kristen wonder what wasn't being said.

Ellie instantly filled in the blanks. "Austin brought a girl a couple of years ago who lectured us on the cruelty of freeze branding."

"Guess she's never seen hot branding."

"She hadn't seen *anything*. Austin spent more time calming her down, than helping out. Finally, she sat in the truck and ignored us all."

"Interesting." She meant that sincerely.

"But you guys aren't…" Ellie made a gesture with the clipboard as if encouraging Kristen to set her straight one way or the other.

"No." Kristen gave her head a quick shake. "He's friends with my twin sister and things just worked out for him to give me a ride to Salt Lake."

"Are you going to watch him ride there?"

"I'm catching the bus the rest of the way home."

"To Marietta."

"Yes."

Ellie frowned at her and seemed about to say something, then instead she nodded at Kristen's shirt. "Do you want something old and beat up to wear over that?"

"I probably won't hurt it manning the clipboard."

Ellie arched an eyebrow. "You've been to how many brandings?"

Kristen smiled—a genuine smile that made her feel lighter inside. "Right. If you have something I'll borrow it."

"*If* I have something. Dear heavens." She jerked her head toward the house, then moved toward the side-by-side ATV. "Come on. My Aunt Katherine is still at the house and I promised to give her a ride to the corrals. You can pick a grubby jacket, and by the time we're back, the guys will be ready to start moving calves through the chute." Ellie gave her a wry smile. "And you can meet Duane."

"Duane?"

"The world's yappiest dog and the center of my aunt's universe."

KRISTEN'S MOTHER HAD grown up on the Marvell Cattle Company ranch, so Austin wasn't surprised to see that Kristen was very much at home at the chutes, wearing one of Clinton's old denim jackets and jotting information on the clipboard. What did surprise him was that she and Ellie acted like old friends.

But, like Whitney, Ellie had never met a stranger. And maybe Kristen did better with people who didn't have a preconceived idea about who she was. She was more relaxed than he had ever seen her...unless their gazes met. Then there'd be that little jolt he was certain she felt as much as he did.

A jolt of...what?

He didn't have that pinned down yet, but it kept him thinking as they worked their way through a hundred calves. The three younger guys, Clinton's cousins, pushed the calves through the chute. He and Clinton clamped them onto the calf table, rotated it, taking turns branding and vaccinating. Ellie's Aunt Katherine helped Ellie load the needles while Kristen recorded exactly what vaccinations and medications each animal received.

Midway through the day, they broke for lunch and Katherine got her little poodle dog, Duane, out of the playpen where he'd been barking all day while they worked. Austin didn't know what it was about ranchers and small yappy dogs, but he knew a lot of bona fide ranch guys who carried the little beasts around on one arm. He didn't get it.

When he left the AEBR tour and got a dog, it would be a real dog. A dog with some size to him and some baritone to his voice. Duane had a high-pitched yip that made Austin's shoulders go tight every time he heard it. And he heard it a lot that day.

After the break, they went back to the branding. Kristen was all business as she did her job. He knew because he didn't seem to be able to keep himself from watching her. Clinton caught him a couple of times and gave him a look that clearly said, "You sure you're only traveling together?"

Austin kept his mouth shut, because he knew the dangers of protesting too much. But the truth of the matter was that he was surprised that Kristen seemed to fit in with his friends. She fit in better than Sierra had a couple years ago…and maybe that was it. Anyone would have fit in after Sierra's behavior that day. It wasn't the last time he'd dated an urbanite, but it was the last time he'd brought one to a ranch.

Now he was here with Kristen, whom he wasn't dating at all, but who kept drawing his eye, just as she had in high school. This was different though. He was studying her because he was trying to figure her out. She didn't mind being touched, but she wasn't used to it. That's what she said anyway. Yeah. It had him thinking.

"Any time now," Clinton said.

He brought his attention back to the calf, slid the needle under the skin on his neck and pushed the plunger.

"Four more," Clinton said as they tipped the table together. The calf had a low tag number—one of the first born that season. Heavy guy.

"I could use a beer," Austin muttered.

"Or four."

He laughed. "Maybe not four. Three. I'm in training."

Clinton grunted an acknowledgment just as Katherine let out a shriek.

"Get him!" Ellie yelled, pointing toward the white streak heading straight for the pen where the cows were mothering up with their babies. "Those ladies will stomp him into the mud."

Austin doubted that 'those ladies'—the cows—could catch him, but if they got lucky, Katherine would be inconsolable. Both he and Clinton dived for the dog, who swerved away, and the last thing he saw before going down was Kristen dropping her clipboard. A split second later a cheer went up, and he raised his head to see Kristen lying on her stomach in the dirt, her hand wrapped firmly around squirming Duane's hind leg.

She was instantly surrounded by a crowd—Ellie helping her up, Katherine scooping up Duane and nuzzling him and then throwing an arm around Kristen and hugging her close. Clinton smiling and helping her brush off—although some of the stuff she'd landed in didn't brush easily. Only Austin and the teenage boys in the pens didn't mob her. But across the distance their gazes locked, and then she looked back at Katherine, who was trying to hug her again. Austin went back to the table, groaned as he tipped it upright and released the calf.

Kristen laughing—genuinely laughing—was an amazing sight. She was covered in cow shit from the knees down and her chin was dirty from where it had hit the dirt, but she looked beautiful.

Austin shook his head and motioned for the boys to bring the next calf down the chute. He'd thought his days of having Kristen Alexander stir things deep inside of him were long gone.

Apparently, he'd been mistaken.

BRANDINGS AT THE Callahan Ranch always ended with a big dinner. Both Clinton and Ellie had put in a day's work getting the meal ready so that all components could be pulled out of the oven, the fridge, or microwaved with the least amount of effort when the tired crew returned to the house.

Katherine took over the kitchen while everyone else washed up and then settled in the living room with much-needed beer. Kristen changed her clothes, politely refusing Ellie's offer to wash her jeans, and then disappeared into the kitchen with Katherine. When she didn't come back, Austin went in to find her washing the roasting pan while Katherine made gravy.

"Need help?"

Kristen gave him a look over her shoulder while Katherine said briskly, "You shoo on out of here. We have everything under control."

Austin allowed himself to be shooed out of the kitchen and rejoined the crew in the living room. He didn't know if Kristen was hiding or making herself useful, but she appeared comfortable where she was and who was he to interfere?

There was just one thing that he hadn't counted on and he had a feeling Kristen wasn't going to be that happy after he told her. He waited until the dishwasher was loaded, the extra dishes done and every freaking surface in the house had been wiped down before he ambled over to where she was draining the sink and asked if he could speak to her outside.

Instantly cautious, she followed him out the door.

"I don't know how to say this, so I'm just going to jump right in." Her eyes rounded with alarm, so he hurried to say, "Nothing earth-shattering. It's just that there's no room for…us…" meaning her "…in the house. Katherine has the spare bedroom."

He'd been offered the bedroom on every single branding he'd attended on the Callahan Ranch, but had always slept in his bedroll in the truck. Now, the one time he'd counted on the spare bedroom, Katherine had come to visit. Apparently, Ellie had just assumed he'd be arriving alone and following his usual custom. Which was fine…as long as Kristen was okay with it.

Not that she had a lot of choice.

"The boys are bedding down in the living room," he added when she didn't respond immediately.

"I see."

Austin cleared his throat. "I'm sleeping in the bed of the truck."

"Where am *I* sleeping?" she asked in a grim voice.

"Well…in the bed of the truck."

She put up her hands. "Unacceptable."

"We can sleep head to toe."

She grimaced and he had to admit, sleeping with someone's feet in your face didn't sound all that inviting.

"Sleep face to face."

No grimace, but she didn't look at all happy with the idea. "I'm sorry about this. I didn't know Katherine would be here."

"I understand." She folded her arms over her chest, looked toward the Dodge, then back at him. "I can sleep in the back seat of the truck."

"How?" It was a reasonable question. Kristen was almost as tall as he was.

"I'll scrunch."

"Sleep in the bed with me and I'll build a divider."

"A divider." She rolled her eyes. "I don't want a divider. I just don't want to sleep with you." Her mouth tightened. "You know what I mean."

She didn't want to have sex with him. That was very clear. "You want to pick who you sleep with. I mean sleep literally. I get that."

"I'll sleep on the back seat."

"Suit yourself."

Chapter Six

ELLIE GAVE KRISTEN blankets after she confessed that she'd "forgotten" her sleeping bag. Later, after she and Austin had excused themselves, she arranged the blankets on the rear seat while Austin rolled out his canvas bedroll. After climbing into the back seat and closing the door, she stretched out as far as she could. It was tight, but she tended to sleep on her side anyway. Except that the seat was just *that much* too short and *that much* too narrow. She could open the door and let her feet hang out. Yes. That was one solution. Awkward, but doable.

"Sure you don't want to come back here?" Austin asked about five minutes after she'd opened the door—possibly because the dome light wouldn't go off and it was keeping them both awake. And running down the battery.

"Fine." Kristen got out of the truck and pulled on the blankets, bundling them into her arms and then carting them to the rear of the truck, where she dumped them unceremoniously on the open tailgate.

"Want me to build the divider?"

"Bite me," she muttered, sounding more like Whitney

than herself as she climbed in to the truck bed. She stretched out on top of his canvas bedroll, pulling the blankets up over her. The canvas made a decent barrier and since she was fully clothed, it wasn't that cold. Really.

It felt so good to stretch her legs all the way out that she was willing to put up with a little cold.

"And thank you for not asking me where to bite," she said as Austin rolled over, presenting his back to her.

"Saving that for later."

"Right." She snuggled deeper into her blankets, wishing he hadn't said that. What would it be like to be nipped with those very white teeth? Her stomach tightened as a warmth unfurled deep inside of her. Even on top of the canvas, she was too close to the man, and it didn't help matters that she really loved the way he smelled. But she was not sleeping head to feet. That would be admitting defeat.

Da head. Da feet. Hahaha.

She was losing it.

Kristen sucked in a breath, thought back to saner times, when she wasn't sharing the bed of a truck with a bull rider, when she'd had a nine-to-five job. When she was traveling along her planned trajectory. Amazing how one unplanned event could throw everything off track so effectively. And try as she might to get things back on track, nothing seemed to work. The loss of perceived control was devastating to her world view.

'Perceived' being the key word. Yes, you could do all the

planning in the world, but shit happened…and you ended up sleeping in the back of a truck with a bull rider who was more attractive than he had any business being.

What was a person supposed to do?

Suck it up. Roll with the punches.

Easy to say, hard to do, but she couldn't keep living as she was, on the edge of anxiety, ashamed of the fact that she'd failed. She needed to get some perspective.

She needed to stop feeling as if she wanted to snuggle closer to Austin, and not just for warmth.

Really…what would that get her?

Answers to questions she'd once wondered about…questions she was still wondering about.

Sometimes it was best not to know; not to add new complexities into a life she was already having a hard time managing.

"Kristen?" Austin spoke softly, but his voice sounded overly loud in the quiet desert night.

"Yes?"

"Go to sleep."

How, when she was so damned aware of him that her entire body was throbbing? She let out a long breath. "I'm trying."

"Try harder."

He rolled over so that his face was close to hers. She felt the warmth coming off him, the warm scent rising from the bedroll he was enveloped in. Felt like leaning in. Getting closer.

A shiver went through her and it wasn't because of the cold.

"Austin…"

"Yeah?"

"It feels really crazy to be here like this."

"It must be like a dream come true."

Laughter bubbled up at his ridiculous statement and escaped her lips before she could stop it. She cleared her throat.

"You can laugh, you know. It's okay. It doesn't mean you've lost control of a situation."

His comment stopped her cold. Was she that transparent? Or was he that intuitive? Did it matter which, when he'd hit the nail on the head?

"You might be right." Why not admit it? It was true. There was a brief silence, then she said, "Are you going to tell me to be more like my sister?"

"Do you hear that a lot?"

"Practically never, actually."

Austin rolled over on his back and stared up at the stars. "Do you want to be more like Whit?"

"I…want to break free a little."

"Just a little?"

Her voice was small when she said, "A lot. I want to break all the habits I've developed over the years. I want to say screw it, and do what I want and not care about what people think."

And there it was in a nutshell. She'd spent way too much time in her life worrying about what other people thought. What their perceptions were. It wasn't how she wanted to live.

He said nothing. Kristen rolled over onto her back, mirroring his position, flopping an arm over her forehead.

"And you're right," she murmured. "About laughing."

"You were laughing today. After catching Duane."

"That was different."

"How?"

She let out a sigh. She couldn't articulate how it was different, but it was. Not everything had to be placed in a specific box. The thought had no sooner entered her head than she realized how out of character it was for her. She loved her boxes.

She lay back down, watching a meteor streak across the sky. Unfettered. Free. And perhaps close to crashing and burning. The thought made her give another small shudder. Crashing and burning was no fun, but freedom… Might it be worth the risk? She'd already crashed and burned.

And never wanted to do it again.

She closed her eyes, but they flashed open when Austin dropped a lazy arm over her.

"Give me your back." His voice was low and close to her ear, sending another shiver through her.

"Excuse me?" Her voice was thick.

"Roll over so your back is to me. We'll spoon through

miles of canvas. You'll be warmer because of it and maybe…just maybe…you might fall asleep."

Kristen opened her mouth to protest, then thought, 'Screw it.' He was right. She needed more warmth and he needed his sleep.

She turned her back to him and he pulled her closer. The canvas of his bedroll bunched between them. She pulled in a breath, let out a sigh as her muscles relaxed. It didn't feel bad, having Austin at her back.

Crazy, crazy times.

Snuggled up to a bull rider in the middle of the desert.

She hadn't seen this one coming.

KRISTEN WOKE WITH a start, rising on one elbow and pushing her hair back with her free hand as she tried to remember where she was, why she was outdoors. Why she was no longer soaring through the air, as she'd been doing just seconds before.

The stirring behind her brought her crashing back to earth. She wasn't flying *over* the valley. She was *in* the valley, in the bed of a pickup truck, the crisp April air nipping at her.

With a bull rider snuggled up against her rear end.

She was half afraid to look over her shoulder at Austin, who would, no doubt, be the picture of early morning male sexiness. She wasn't yet ready to face such a thing.

She had no choice.

"Finally," Austin murmured as if it were approaching noon. Since the sun hadn't yet cleared the horizon, she didn't believe that was the case.

"What time are we leaving?"

"Right after coffee." He smiled a little, his eyes crinkling at the corners as if she amused him.

"What are you smiling at?"

"You look kind of good all rumpled."

"Rumpled. Thank you."

"It was a compliment." He didn't smile, but his voice was low and intimate. Warm and seductive. Kristen barely kept herself from swallowing.

Right. A compliment.

He put a hand on her shoulder then and drew her back down, so that they were once again face to face, as they'd been the night before, only now she could see his face clearly. His eyes were so damned blue—blue with white streaks that made them seem even bluer. And his mouth…she allowed her gaze to slide down and hold on his perfectly carved lips.

She needed to think of something else. Immediately.

"Those things I said last night—"

He put his fingertips on her lips, startling her into silence.

"Don't backslide on me, Kristen."

"Hey, you guys! Coffee!"

Kristen let out an audible breath at Ellie's yell and Austin scowled…as if he honestly wanted to continue the conversation. Why?

She wanted to ask him, but the words froze in her throat. Thankfully, Ellie gave another shout from the house.

"We'd better move," she said.

"Yeah." His expression told her that he thought she was engaging in avoidance tactics. She saw it differently. What she was avoiding was none of his business, and she felt massively self-conscious…no…she felt *vulnerable* about the things she'd said yesterday. This morning. She'd revealed her weak spots.

Austin rolled his bedroll while Kristen folded her borrowed blankets and carried them back to the house.

Ellie smiled at Kristen. "I hope you weren't too uncomfortable last night. I don't usually make my guests sleep in the truck."

"Actually, it was very comfortable." Except for the ways in which it wasn't, which had nothing to do with the sleeping arrangements. She was still marveling at the things she'd told Austin. Half regretting them. It'd been the darkness and the intimate setting and the fact that there was something inherently seductive about Austin. That 'something' had threatened her back in the day when she'd found him so tempting that she had to make certain he kept his distance, and it was threatening her now.

It was also making her very, very curious about a lot of

things she had no business being curious about.

IT WAS STILL early when she and Austin drove north to I80, the sun stretching its rays across the pale blue and lavender desert, and glinting off the sagebrush on Kristen's side of the truck. It was a beautiful morning—one of those rare mornings where she actually felt a small stirring of hope. She'd had a good time yesterday. Better than she could have imagined. For a short period of time she'd forgotten about all the crap in her life and simply existed in the moment.

A rare occurrence for her.

"You seemed to hit it off well with Ellie."

"I like her." Ellie had an easy way about her that made Kristen feel as if she'd known her for years. Clinton was the same. How was it that intense Austin had such laid-back friends?

"What happens when we hit Salt Lake City?" Austin reached out to take his sunglasses off the dash and put them on one-handed as they turned onto the freeway and started driving into the sun.

She'd been wondering the same thing. She imagined that she could talk Austin into letting her bunk with him for the night and then beg Whitney to forgive her and drive down to get her. It was a seven-hour drive, so they'd have to spend the night, and it really wasn't fair of her to ask that of her sister under the circumstances—

"I have a proposition for you."

She gave him a slow look, doing her best to ignore the mental picture that the word "proposition" inspired. "What's that?" she asked in a remarkably normal voice. She was getting better at this.

"If you would like to stay with me until after the event, I'll give you a ride to Marietta."

Red flags started waving wildly. "Why would you do that?"

"I have two weeks off after this event. I have a few commitments the second week, but I figured I could visit my brother on the Forty-Six Ranch the first few days off."

She was immediately cognizant of a strange mixture of relief and disappointment. "So this has nothing to do with me."

He glanced over at her, tipping down the sunglasses with one hand so that she could see the very serious expression in his very blue eyes. "It has everything to do with you."

Her heart stuttered.

"How?" Her voice sounded nowhere near normal now.

He brought his gaze back to the road. "The choice is entirely yours. I'm just offering you this opportunity."

"That doesn't answer my question."

He glanced back at her, but she could no longer read his expression because the sunglasses were once again in place. "You told me you wanted to break free. I'm giving you the opportunity to do something different."

Kristen's back stiffened. Yes. One of the things she'd said under cover of darkness that she now regretted. "It's not your job to help me do that."

"Agreed."

And that was all he said, which was way more effective than an argument. His offer was…nuts. And tempting. Her carved-in-stone strategies were no longer working. She needed to be flexible, but she was afraid to be flexible. He knew that. He also knew that she was competitive.

Several days with Austin Harding. Did she dare?

She'd spent so much of her life not daring and what had it gotten her?

Austin eventually broke the silence as they started across the Bonneville Salt Flats, where the earth shone startlingly white in contrast with the ultra-blue sky. "You were different yesterday. And this morning."

"I felt different," she conceded. "And I felt comfortable with your friends."

"I think you should work toward feeling that way all the time." His voice dropped ever so slightly. "Unless you want to settle for safety?"

She studied his profile. "It sounds like you're drawing a line in the sand."

"You seem to do well with lines."

Yes, but she tended to box herself in with them instead of crossing them. "So essentially you're—"

"Challenging you to hang out with me until after my ride? I am. Then I'll drive you to Marietta."

"Will we share a room?"

"Yes."

"But not a bed." She needed to clear that up. She wasn't ready to share a bed with the man, even though she essentially already had.

He looked at her in a way that made a small tremor ripple through her midsection. "Not unless both parties are agreeable."

It was kind of hard to find her voice after that.

"Two beds," he clarified when she didn't respond. "Because I know I make you jumpy." One corner of his mouth tilted up as he quoted her. "What do you say?"

Tough choice. She had the option of heading home to her safety net or she could take a short walk on the wild side. She was due. She was with a guy whom she could now talk to without freezing up. Maybe she could discover a few things about herself.

Maybe it wouldn't hurt her one bit to take a short vacay from reality.

She told her sane inner self, who was now shouting her head off, to shut up. She'd eventually go home. Confess. Take her medicine.

But first…she would hang with a bull rider and see what she was made of.

Her heart beat just a little faster as, for once in her life, she stepped off into the deep end.

"I accept."

Chapter Seven

KRISTEN DIDN'T SAY much as Austin drove through the snarled Salt Lake City traffic to the hotel he'd booked, but he had a pretty good idea of what was going on in her head. Had she made a mistake? Should she stay with him? Shouldn't she? Which was why, after he parked in the long valet line, he turned to her and asked, "Still okay with this?"

"Yes." Her chin tilted up and she was making a brave attempt to look certain in her decision, but he could almost see the mental battle continuing. He'd expected as much. He made her jumpy after all.

And he wanted to know why.

"Why did you decide to give me a ride home?" she asked as he inched the truck forward.

He took the rig out of gear. The valet line was long and slow-moving. "You mean what do I get out of it?"

"Yes."

He debated degrees of honesty, then decided on the whole truth. "I guess I kind of want to see the real you." Her eyebrows drew together in a slow frown. "You know…the person I woke up with this morning? No barriers?"

"Why?" The word came out on a husky note.

He gave a casual shrug. "I had this theory about the 'real' you back in high school. Of course, you blew it all to hell, but I'm beginning to wonder if I was right after all." When he glanced over at her, she was staring at him.

"You're doing research on me?"

He laughed and then reached out to touch her, even though he'd promised not to, lightly brushing the hair away from her cheek. For once she didn't jump or jerk away. "I want to satisfy my curiosity." His expression softened. "I want to get to know you. That's all."

"All right."

Kristen intrigued him. She always had, and despite everything, or maybe because of everything, she still did. And maybe he needed to be honest about that with both of them.

"You're free to call your sister at any time to come rescue you. I'll pay for the gas."

"Or I can stay for the event and then you can run me home, as promised."

He smiled a little, then moved the truck forward again. "You're saying you're up for a little research?"

"As long as we take it slow."

"Honey," he said with a lift of his eyebrows, "I'm a master at taking it slow."

Her lips parted as the meaning of his comment became clear to her and the air slowly eased out of his lungs as he focused in on her soft, lush mouth. A horn honked behind him and they both jumped. He put the truck in gear moved forward into the two empty car lengths ahead of them. A few minutes later they'd reached the front of the line. He surrendered his keys and hefted Kristen's suitcases and his gear over the side of the truck. A bellman loaded it on a cart, then followed them into the swanky lobby.

Austin checked in and, since he'd won a good chunk of change in Reno, he splurged and got a premier room—two queen beds. View of the mountains. High floor. Rooms were in demand due to the bull riders being in town and the prices were jacked up accordingly, but he figured this was kind of a vacation for Kris, and he didn't mind plush digs one bit.

He went back to where Kristen was now standing, hand shading her eyes as she studied the mountains through the tinted window. She dropped her arm as he approached and handed her a keycard.

"Hope you aren't afraid of heights. We're on an upper floor."

"Good. I like looking at the mountains." She met his eyes, her expression serene. Too serene. Faking-it serene. Which meant he'd rattled her in the truck and she was making an effort to cover—but she hadn't crawled back into her shell. She hadn't gone cold.

Once they were in the room and the bellman had been tipped, Kristen went to the window and took another long look at the mountains. Marshaling her defenses? Or admiring the view? When she turned back, Austin said, "Want to set some ground rules?"

She nodded. "Probably a good idea."

"I'll go first." He folded his arms over his chest. "No hogging the bathroom."

She smiled a little. "No gratuitous nudity."

His eyebrows lifted. "I'll keep my clothes on if you do the same."

"I appreciate it. My roommate's previous boyfriend never wore clothes." She cleared her throat. "I…uh…got tired of being startled all the time."

"Understandable." And he couldn't say he liked the idea of a naked guy wandering around her apartment.

"He was a nice guy," Kristen offered. "Just…very comfortable with his body."

"Wasn't trying to get a three-way going?"

After a moment's thought, Kristen said, "No. I really don't think so." She met his gaze. "Ice princess, remember?"

"Some guys like a challenge."

He saw her throat move as she swallowed. "Like you?"

"Yeah. Like me." He dropped his arms. "Any other rules other than bathroom hogging and nudity?"

"I can't think of any. You?"

He took a step forward as he spoke, peeling his watch off his arm and dropping it on the desk. Kristen held her ground, because there still yards of carpet between them, but he had the feeling she wanted to step back. "Just one. Honesty."

"What do you mean?"

"I mean that we talk honestly about what we want and don't want so this doesn't turn into the vacation from hell for you. Or me."

"That's a good rule," she murmured.

"Can you do it? Be honest with me and not clam up?"

Her chin tilted up. "I can try."

He nodded. "Good. Because I'm going to call you on it if you don't."

"What's your schedule?"

"I'll be working out. Seeing a trainer and doing my physical therapy. I have a sponsor's event on Thursday. Prelims on Friday and finals on Saturday."

"We go home on Sunday."

"That we do."

Kristen sank down on the edge of the bed closest to the window. "If you don't mind me asking, what are you going home to?"

Reasonable question, since his family had literally lost the farm when he was a teen and after he'd graduated high school, his parents had moved to Arizona. He had no home in Marietta, but he had a brother living on the Forty-Six Ranch with his new bride.

"My brother has a trailer on the ranch that he lets me use."

"So, no home."

"Nope."

"You have no home at all?"

The idea seemed to perplex her. "I'm a drifter."

"What do you do during the off-season?"

"You mean October to December? Those three months? I find a place to train. Usually down south. Oklahoma or Texas."

"No home."

He gave a shrug. "What can I say? I don't need one yet."

"But you will someday." When he didn't answer, she added, "You can't drift forever…right?"

"Probably not." But the days of him not drifting were in the distant future. In the meantime, he banked as much money as possible, paid some crazy insurance rates for catastrophic care with a super high deductible. A lot of guys didn't have any insurance at all, but he didn't want to completely drain his savings if he had a run of bad luck.

"What will you do after bull riding?"

"Another good question."

She narrowed her eyes at him, as if suspecting that he was putting her on. He wasn't, and after a moment, she said, "You have no plans?"

"When I need a plan, I'll come up with one."

"Wow." He half expected a lecture, but instead she rose to her feet and said, "You are the antithesis of me."

He almost said, "Opposites attract?" but didn't want to push things. "Want to grab dinner tonight?"

"About that. I'm going to pay you back for my half of this vacation from reality."

"You think?" He issued the words as a soft challenge.

Kristen met it head on. "I know."

AUSTIN HEADED TO the gym while Kristen unpacked her suitcase. She'd overstuffed the bag and hated leaving things all crammed together and wrinkled. Austin had assured her that she could have the entire wardrobe, and she took him at his word, filling the drawers and hanging her blouses and jackets.

One suitcase didn't carry that much, so her wardrobe would be limited for the next few days, but if she really got desperate, she could wear her interview suit. She smiled at the thought. After unpacking, she paced the room, glancing first at the panoramic view of the mountains, then at Austin's bed. Was she crazy to do this?

If so, then why did it feel so right? And why did she feel so different? Her short time on the Callahan Ranch had been so radically different from her 'real' life that she'd acted like a different person. Especially after eating dirt while trying to catch the renegade poodle.

It'd been the lack of expectations from the people there, she'd decided on the tail end of the drive to Salt Lake, after she'd told Austin that she'd stay with him. They didn't know her or expect her to be perfect, so she could be…not perfect.

It had felt like being on the Marvell Ranch with her cousins…except that Austin didn't feel like a cousin. Far from it.

She sat on the edge of her bed, staring out over the mountains that towered over the city. It honestly felt right being here. She hoped it still felt right in the coming days. And if it didn't, she could go home.

She didn't see that happening.

Reaching over to the nightstand, she unplugged her phone from the charger and dialed up Whitney. It was late afternoon, so she was probably working her shift at Flint-Works, but at least she would see that her sister had called and wouldn't be able to accuse her of keeping her uninformed. But to Kristen's surprise, her twin answered.

"Where are you?"

"Salt Lake City."

"You'll be home tomorrow?"

"No…I'll be home on Sunday."

"Sunday?"

"I'm staying with Austin Harding. He'll drive me to Marietta after his event."

"You mean his bull-riding event?"

"Exactly."

There was a long silence on the other end of the phone, then Whitney said in a cautious voice, "Who are you and what have you done with my sister?"

"Your sister," Kristen said in a patient voice, "is trying to get her act together."

"By sleeping with a bull rider? I mean Austin is hot and all, but this seems very out of character for you. Besides that…since when do you two get along?"

"I'm not sleeping with him." Yet. She had a feeling it was coming, but she wanted things to unfold naturally.

There was a long silence, during which Kristen rolled her eyes to the ceiling, studied the textured panels there. "I'm very confused," Whitney finally said. "Maybe you should start at the beginning?"

"That's a long story," Kristen said on a sigh.

"And I have lots of time."

"Aren't you on shift?"

"Schedule change. I'm at home with not a lot to do. Therefore, I think you should spill your guts."

Kristen arranged a pillow behind her head and spilled. It took some time to answer all of Whitney's questions, and assure her sister that she hadn't gone off the deep end. Surely everyone deserved an escape from brutal reality— unemployment, unconfessed sins?

After Whitney's cross-examination ended, she fell silent. To the point that Kristen said her name, fearing that the call had been dropped.

"I'm here. Just digesting everything."

"What's the verdict?" Kristen wasn't so much looking for approval as understanding.

"Don't go super crazy."

"I can go a little crazy?" It was supposed to be a joke, but it didn't feel like a joke. And Whitney didn't take it that way.

She drew in an audible breath and then said, "Consider consequences, but don't let fear rule your life."

Kristen closed her eyes as her twin's words sank in. "Do you think I've let fear rule my life?"

"Totally."

She didn't say anything, because it was so very true. She was a freaking coward, judging her self-worth by the reactions of others.

"There's a middle ground, Kris. Find it."

"I might need some help."

"When you get home, I'll give you lessons on flaunting authority and not caring about what other people think."

Kristen gave a soft laugh, feeling better now that she was once again connected with her sister. It'd been stupid to keep her in the dark about her job, but that damned pride thing.

And the fear thing.

"Any more advice?" Kristen asked.

"Practice safe sex?"

Kristen's body went warm. "Sex isn't on the agenda." And if it was, she wasn't going to share with her sister. She felt possessive about this time away from her real life. Any decisions she made were her own, as were any consequences.

Whitney gave a soft laugh. "You might want to rethink

that."

KRISTEN WAS IN bed with the lights turned out on her side of the room when Austin got back to the hotel room after working out and then grabbing a quick bite with Kane, who'd also shown up early. He had a suspicion his roomie was still awake, but she didn't say a word, so he returned the favor.

He'd showered at the gym, so it was a matter of shucking out of his jeans and rolling into bed once the lights were out. Not that he was going to sleep yet. He pulled out his phone, plugged in the headphones and started pulling up videos of both his past rides and the bull he'd be paired with at the upcoming event. His body creaked a little as he shifted positions periodically and he wondered about taking another dose of anti-inflammatory pills, then decided to muscle through. He'd barely put his phone aside when Kristen spoke, her voice drifting through the darkness.

"Tell me about bull riding."

The question surprised him, coming out of nowhere as it did. "What about it?"

"Anything."

He put a hand behind his head, the movement making him aware of his sore shoulder. "I get on. Hope the bull doesn't throw anything my way that I can't counter." He wasn't sure how much she wanted to hear. She wasn't like the buckle bunnies, who wanted to hear anything he said in order to carve another notch in their figurative bedpost.

"Why bulls? Why not become a calf roper? Or a bronc rider?"

"Maybe because Ty is a bronc rider and he's damned good at it, and someone accused me of being a loser, so I decided to become the best at something."

Kristen didn't answer immediately and when she did, she sounded suspicious. "Really?"

"Let's say that moment caused me to think about things differently. I was never a loser. I had a plan. It just didn't involve school. But after you, I took that plan a whole lot more seriously."

"So you owe me."

He gave a low laugh. "I would have been a champion regardless."

"You're certain?"

"Champions run in the family." Which was true, although his dad had given up his promising rodeo career to farm and the decision had made him a bitter man after he lost the land he'd sacrificed for—which was why he lived through his two sons. He was proud as hell of Ty, who was the subject of a documentary, and prouder still of Austin, who was still out on the road, keeping the family name squarely in the limelight.

Heaven help him when he was no longer doing that. A

bull rider didn't have a long career, and what was his dad going to do when both of his sons retired?

Austin never let those thoughts hang for too long. As it was, his dad could be a royal pain while in his stage-father persona. If he didn't have his sons to brag about and try to micromanage from a distance…again, Austin didn't want to think about it.

"You make a lot of money at this?"

"I have this season."

"And you risk death while you do it."

It was a fact all bull riders lived with.

"Do you really consider this a serious career?"

"I do. The most serious you can imagine."

"But you have no plans afterward."

They'd covered this territory. He wasn't in the mood to cover it again. But he did like talking to Kris, and maybe it was best that they end on a good note. "My plans right now involve sleeping so that I'm at the top of my game."

"I understand." He heard the sheets rustle as she rolled over in bed, and he found himself wishing that he was in the bed with her. Just to spoon her up against him, if nothing else.

Spooning wouldn't be enough.

But it would be a start…

"Good night, Kristen."

There was a wistful note to her voice, almost enough to make him cross the distance to her bed, when she said,

"Good night, Austin."

THE NEXT MORNING, he woke up with morning wood straining against his boxers. Kristen's bed was empty, and the shower was running. He closed his eyes, idly rubbing his hand over the length of his hard-on through his underwear. It would be advisable to *not* have a hard-on when he got out of bed—either that or to get out of bed when Kristen wasn't around—but envisioning naked Kristen on the other side of the wall, water cascading over her body, wasn't doing him a lot of good.

In fact, it was doing him no good.

He grabbed for the remote, turned on the news and laced his hands behind his head. Couldn't focus.

Get it together, man.

He had a sense of honor, after all. He'd asked Kristen to share a room, not a bed, and he wasn't going to push things by walking around with an erection.

He focused mightily on the television after the shower stopped. Government budget. Yes. Oh, a bridge had some rusty welds. Imagine that. A man with a rat riding on his head was seen multiple times on the streets of Salt Lake City. Interesting.

The door opened and steam rolled out. The hair dryer came on.

Austin started to relax. He figured from past experience that the dryer could go on for a long time, especially with long hair like Kristen's, so he took a chance and pushed back the covers—just as Kristen stepped out of the bathroom, hair dryer still in hand, looking as if she was going to ask him a question.

Whatever she'd been about to say died on her lips as she caught sight of full-blown *him.*

"Oh."

Austin yanked the sheet over his tented boxers. "Sorry. I was going for my jeans."

She gave a quick nod and retreated into the bathroom, leaving Austin feeling very much the fool. He reached for his jeans, dragged them up his legs.

"I'll give more warning next time," Kristen called from the bathroom over the noise of the dryer.

"I thought you were used to naked men." Austin rolled his eyes as soon as he finished speaking. There were better face-saving remarks, but he couldn't come up with one. And technically he hadn't been naked.

"Flaccid ones."

The matter-of-fact remark had his eyebrows shooting up. *Okay.*

The dryer shut off and he heard it clatter onto the counter. "I'm coming out."

"All clear," Austin said dryly.

She peeked around the corner, then stepped out into full

view, wearing a satiny robe that clung to her curves. He glanced down at his bare chest and then reached for his shirt on the chair near his bed. "I'll work harder at this nudity thing." Although her robe wasn't doing that great of a job of hiding her assets.

"I don't mind bare chests."

"I see." He pulled the shirt on, but stopped short of snapping it. Kristen not only didn't mind bare chests—she seemed to be somewhat fascinated with his.

"You have a lot of scars."

"Part of the game."

She shook her head and went to the closet to pull clothing out of a drawer. She'd unpacked, just as she said she was going to. And then she was going to have to pack again. Austin had a great method for avoiding both of those steps, but apparently Kristen wasn't the yank-it-out-of-the-suitcase and cram it back in kind of person.

No big surprise there.

"I'm going to dress around the corner. The bathroom is too damp."

"How about I go into the bathroom and you can dress where it's dry."

She gave a jerky nod, his first indication that she was feeling self-conscious. "Great idea. Thank you."

He grabbed his toiletry kit off the bureau on the way to the john. "I'll give a yell before I come out."

She clutched the clothing she held to her chest. "Thank

you."

Austin then closed the door, trapping himself in a room filled with feminine smells—hair products, body spray. Kristen's makeup bag lay open on the counter and he peeked inside as he unzipped his jeans.

High-end stuff, judging from the containers. She was a high-end kind of woman.

Who was no stranger to calf brandings and ranch work.

You're not going to figure her out. You don't need to figure her out.

He didn't. Any more than she needed to figure him out—although he was pretty much an open book. Bull rider. Drifter. Lover of a good time.

Now he was a bull rider who'd given her something of a gift—a few days in which she didn't really need to worry about anything—except for catching her roommate in a state of arousal.

When he came out of the bathroom, Kristen was sitting on her bed, which was neatly made. Austin cocked an eyebrow.

"I wanted to sit on it."

"All right…" It made no sense to him. He sat in the chair near the window and pulled on first his socks and then his new Tony Lama boots. Loved his boots. Custom-made and comfy. When he finished pulling the second boot on, he looked up to see Kristen studying him as if debating options.

He got to his feet, gathered his change and his watch,

stuffed his wallet into his pocket, then grabbed his gym bag. "I'm heading to the gym, then I have a meeting."

"I thought I might take in the sights for an hour or two."

All very polite and businesslike, as if he hadn't waved an erection at her earlier that morning. He gestured to the door. "I'll buy you a coffee?"

"Sure." She gathered her purse, pulled her sweater off the back of a chair and then followed him out of the room and down the hall to the elevators, all of which seemed to be permanently stuck on lower floors.

Austin rocked back on his heels as they waited. "Interesting morning."

Kristen let out a tiny huff of breath, which he took as an acknowledgment. He gave her a sideways look. "Still okay with our arrangement?"

Her lips parted as she gave him a speculative look. "I am. I went into this to ease out of my comfort zone, and I'd say this morning was a start."

"Good start or bad?"

"Still working on that one."

He smiled a little as the elevator doors finally opened. They stepped inside and the doors closed, then the elevator started up instead of heading down. Two floors up the doors slid open and held.

"Maybe we should change elevators," Austin said.

"Yes." But she didn't move. Instead, she pressed her lips together in a thoughtful way, then gave him a look. "I want to tell you something. Explain something."

"Yeah?"

"When we were in high school and that…thing between us happened…one reason I was so upset was because I had a big crush on you."

Austin blinked at her as the elevator doors closed and the car started a slow downward journey. "No fucking way."

"Yeah." She glanced at the parquet floor. "Then you called me an ice princess and made bets about me…it hurt."

His chest squeezed. "Ice princess was kind of a compliment." She gave him a disbelieving look. "Ice troll would have been a slam."

She fought a smile. "Thank you for clarifying."

He smiled back. "Thank you for confessing. It kind of helps me understand the fury of your attack."

"You started it," she pointed out. "And then you came looking for an explanation."

"Yeah. I did." The elevator lurched to a stop. The doors remained stubbornly closed. He didn't care. "I owe you another apology."

"I don't need—" Her words died on her lips as he leaned down to touch his mouth to hers, apologizing in the best way he knew how—a way that might convince her that all of her self-doubts were meaningless where he was concerned. The softness of her lips almost did him in, but he kept himself in check, sliding one hand along her smooth cheek to hold her face steady as he deepened the kiss, keeping his touch on her face light, instead of backing her against the elevator wall as his instincts were urging him to do. Just as Kristen started returning his kiss like she meant it, her tongue finally meeting his, stroking, making him go hard again, the elevator began moving.

"I can't decide if I like this thing or hate it," he murmured, letting his hand drop slowly away from her face, before turning to face the front of the car.

"Nice apology," Kristen murmured.

"Best I could do." The doors slid open, revealing a small crowd waiting on the ground floor.

"This elevator isn't working right," he told the people waiting to get on. They ignored his warning and piled on board. But he had to admit to thinking more about Kristen than possessed elevators. He waited until they'd gotten their coffee and were seated at a small table near the edge of the lobby before saying, "Tell me about this crush."

"To stroke your ego?"

"My ego is big enough, thank you. Why didn't I know? I mean...I tried to talk to you."

Kristen lifted her cup to her lips. "Scared. To. Death."

"Of what? I sent out signals. I thought I did anyway."

"Misreading. Rejection...and..." she glanced down "...the fact that you were going nowhere."

His eyebrows rose and she gave a self-conscious shrug. "I had plans. You didn't. At that time, I thought that every relationship had to be serious. That futures had to mesh.

Things like that."

"What do you think about relationships now?"

"I guess I understand that there are different kinds. Futures don't have to mesh."

"That pretty well describes us—non-meshing futures."

"Yeah."

"Which leaves the question of what kind of relationship do you want to have with me?" It was a question worth asking right off the bat, so there were no misconceptions.

She held his gaze as she said, "The fun kind that leaves no scars."

"Have you ever had one of those?" She shook her head. "Neither have I. The thing is, Kris, you go past a certain point and every relationship stings a little."

"So you're saying…"

"Maybe I shouldn't have kissed you in that elevator."

Chapter Eight

KRISTEN STARED AT Austin for a long moment. She could still feel the pressure of his lips on hers, could still *taste* him. It'd shocked her when he'd leaned in and kissed her, but shock had quickly turned to desire, fueled in part by the hot, disturbing dream she'd had the night before. A dream she could have made a reality by simply crossing the space between their beds.

Why hadn't she crossed?

Fear of rejection. Fear that they weren't on the same page.

Fear was a tough bitch to deal with, but then he'd kissed her, making her realize that her time with him was short, and that she wanted to do what other women did—to go after what she wanted in the personal realm instead of overthinking everything. The sense of freedom and empowerment she'd had since waking up with Austin in the Nevada desert had been growing—was still growing. She wasn't exactly kicking butt and taking names, but she was able to look him square in the eye and say, "I have some social issues, but I can handle life. I can deal with a few bumps and bruises. A scar or two."

"Maybe I can't."

Somehow that didn't ring true. "You were the one who made comments about not sharing beds unless both parties were agreeable."

"Both parties, Kristen."

Rejection.

And it was *a bitch.*

She tilted her chin up, her fingers digging into her palms under the table. She was in too deep to retreat now. There was no way she was coming out of this situation with her pride intact, so she forged on.

"Here's the thing, Austin…it isn't like I chose to be attracted to you, but I am." Her cheeks started to burn, but she was a woman on a mission. "And you kissed me as if you didn't find me lacking." He'd held back in the elevator. She'd been more than aware, and had held back herself, letting him lead the way, even though she'd wanted to melt into him.

She pulled a hand out from under the table and jabbed a finger into the Formica between them. "If you're worried about *me*, you need to stop now. If you're worried about yourself, that's acceptable."

"I'm *not* taking advantage of you while you're on the road with me. That wasn't what I had in mind when I said I'd help you break free."

Her gaze went cold. "Take advantage of me?"

He shrugged.

"I think about you being naked, Austin." Had dreamed about him and woken up feeling damp and frustrated. His eyes narrowed ever so slightly, as if he wasn't sure if she was kidding or not, and she fought to hold his very blue gaze. "I'm not saying I'm ready to tumble into bed at this very moment, but…I think about you naked."

"That's direct."

"That's honest," she said in a low voice. "We agreed to be honest." One of his ground rules. "And in case you're wondering, yes, I'm dying a thousand deaths inside."

"Good to know."

"I understand if you're not ready to make a move, but *you* need to own that. Not pass it off onto me."

"I feel like I'm standing in the hallway in front of your locker."

It took her a second to get his drift. "I have a hard time saying things sometimes, but it doesn't mean I can't do it."

"Obviously."

"It costs me." Total truth.

He studied his hands, which were loosely clasped around his mug of untouched coffee. He frowned a little. "Think about me naked, huh?"

She gave a shrug, thankful that it came off as casual instead of a jerky up and down motion. "You are well built."

He gave a considering nod. "I'm not starting anything I don't feel good about. You aren't going to be my one-night stand."

If she'd walked into a brick wall, it wouldn't have felt more solid than the rejection she'd just received. Perhaps this was why she never hung herself out there before. There was so much opportunity for failure, and she'd never handled failure well. On the other hand, she was at the point now where she had nothing to lose.

"I'm not looking for a commitment, Austin. I'm looking for an adventure."

"When did you decide this?"

"Last night in bed." After she'd woken up hot and bothered, more than aware that adventure was only a few feet away from her.

"Sometimes adventures have a way of getting out of hand." He spoke as if he were very familiar with adventures getting out of hand. "Tell me what you think about this…we keep things on the straight and narrow until I get you back to Marietta? Then we can re-evaluate."

Kristen pressed her lips together. Of course, she had no choice but to say yes, so it surprised her when she said, "My counter offer is that we keep an open mind and see how things play out."

His eyebrows drew together. "We're only here for a couple more days."

"Then time is on your side."

She liked the way he looked at her if his perception of her was crumbling, piece by tiny piece. She knew the feeling.

She was adjusting her own self-perception, discovering that she could do things that usually froze her up. Not easily, but she was starting to hold her own.

He looked her straight in the eye, frowning a little as he said, "I'm not sleeping with you, Kris. Not under these circumstances."

And now she was dealing with not one rejection, but two.

"Does sex ruin your knees?" She couldn't keep the snarky edge out of her voice.

"No. Bull riding hurts my knees and sex exacerbates the injury."

She was losing.

He reached across the table to cover her hands with his and, surprisingly, instead of tensing her up, the warm contact made Kristen's tight muscles give a little. Maybe because she *had* lost and needed to accept failure. His gaze dropped to her lips and held just long enough to make her breath catch. "I'm trying not to do anything either of us will regret."

Kristen gave a slight nod. Hard to argue with that. "What do we do now?"

"We'll follow our ground rules, observe the boundaries. Be friends. Be honest."

"You're sure you're down for the honesty part?"

He smiled a little. "It was my rule, so I guess I have to be."

"Then I'm probably still going to think about you naked, and you can think about me any way you'd like."

THE PRIVACY SIGN was on the door when Kristen got back to hotel later that afternoon, leaving her in a bit of a conundrum. Was he sleeping? Showering? Had he forgotten to take the sign off before leaving the room? She gave a small tap on the door.

"Yeah?"

Okay. Not sleeping. She cracked the door open, but didn't look inside. "Are you decent?" After a long day spent pretending to sight-see while mulling things over in her head—i.e. reverting to form and overthinking—she'd concluded that her best course of action was to save face. Act as if the rejections didn't matter. In fact, they should be celebrated because she'd hung herself out there. Taken a chance and, best of all, survived. She couldn't say that her dignity was intact, but she was still breathing.

And now she was facing her first what-doesn't-kill-you-makes-you-stronger challenge.

"Define decent." He sounded like he was exerting himself as he spoke.

"Wearing pants." Unlike this morning when she'd gotten that inspiring eyeful.

"You're safe." She started through the door. "Kind of."

Her heart jumped, but she continued around the partition. Austin was sitting in the hardback office chair, gripping the foot he held on his muscular thigh and pulling it toward his crotch with both hands. And he *was* wearing pants. Kind of. The spandex bike shorts left little to the imagination.

"Yoga?" Kristen asked as she casually walked by to drop her purse on her bed.

"Nope. Physical therapy stretches." He pulled his foot higher up his thigh as he spoke, gritting his teeth as he did so. "Working on my hip flexors."

"I see."

And boy did she. She saw taut muscles straining against the forces placed upon them. A light sheen of sweat showed on his bare chest and pecs, making the contours of his torso look utterly amazing. She cleared her throat, which was starting to feel dry. "I have some more shopping to do. I'll let you get on with your training."

"You don't have to leave." He grabbed the towel on the back of the chair and slung it over his shoulder. "I'll even put on more clothes."

"You're fine," she said.

He gave her a look.

"I'm used to naked men." Although Lynn's ex had looked nothing like Austin.

"The flaccid kind. I remember," he said dryly. "I'm going to shower and then maybe we can get something to eat before it gets too packed downstairs."

"Sure." She managed a smile. "I'll change while you're in the bathroom."

"You look great the way you are."

She glanced down at her white cotton dress, then back up at him. He shrugged as if her looking good was a no-brainer before turning toward the bathroom.

"In that case, I guess I'll just sit out here and think about you being naked in there." Okay...maybe she hadn't fully moved on from the morning's conversation. She'd do better in the future.

"You're not making this easy," he said as he closed the door.

"Easy wasn't part of the deal."

AUSTIN WAS GLAD he'd been on his way to the john when Kristen tossed out her last remark, because his dick started to thicken as soon as she mentioned thinking about him naked. Spandex was not a good medium for containing a hard-on. In fact, it was one of the worst.

He closed the bathroom door and tipped his head back to look up at the ceiling. Tried to recall his mission. It wasn't to sleep with Kristen.

Was it?

He couldn't see how that was a bad thing, but she was dealing with some shit, and women that were dealing with shit, sometimes made poor choices. As did guys. No need to be sexist.

He'd kissed her on impulse that morning and then regretted it as he started to consider consequences—for Kristen. And when she'd said she wanted fun with no scars, well, that had clinched matters. No screwing around, because how in the hell could he guarantee no scars?

She wanted to mess around…

Her meaning had been more than clear. She wanted an adventure. Scar-free if possible.

Yeah. As if there was such a thing when it came to emotions.

He released his dick from the spandex and worked the black stretchy stuff down his legs, kicking it free before he turned the water on.

They'd go to dinner tonight. Then go to their own beds. Alone. If Kristen had been a casual travel companion, if they didn't have history, and he wasn't friends with her sister, if she wasn't growing on him the way she was, then he might not be so slow to act. But as things were, the situation was ripe for a major fuckup.

Things were certainly a lot easier when Kristen was all frozen up. But he was the guy who'd drawn her out, and now he was the guy who was going to have to make sure he didn't do anything either of them regretted later.

An hour later they were seated at one of the better tables in the hotel restaurant and Austin was determined to keep things on a friendly, personal, but not too personal level.

They ordered drinks and then perused the menu. Kristen ordered a salad. Austin ordered a steak. Then they settled back in their booth and sipped their beer.

"What are your plans after you go home?"

Kristen shrugged. "I'll smooth things over with my parents, and try to find a job."

"In…what? Accounting?"

"That's my degree."

"What made you take the waitress job?" Because even though she looked hot as hell in that costume, Kristen wasn't the waitress type. Or the costume type. He glanced over at her modest cotton dress. Or the show-her-rack type. Her costume had done a good job of that. Her costume had been pretty fucking hot, but that wasn't where his thoughts were supposed to be.

"I was too picky about work the first few weeks after I got laid off. Then I got desperate when I realized that even the minimum-wage jobs were challenging to get, and with my student loans, minimum wage wasn't going to cut it for very long. The Silver Bow paid well and the tips were supposed to be good."

"Supposed to be?"

She smiled ruefully. "I didn't do too well in that regard."

He laughed. "We all have our gifts."

"Yes. Mine is numbers."

"Mine is not."

"You seemed to do okay in math class. You never attended and somehow you passed."

"I attended every now and again." He attended often enough to know about the scar that had identified her to him at the Silver Bow.

She settled her elbows on the table, resting her chin on her hands, her beer sitting essentially untouched. "How did you not get nailed for truancy?"

He also set his elbows on the table, mirroring her. "My dad excused my absences. As long as I was practicing rough stock riding and passing my classes, he was good with anything I did. And I'd like to point out it was not wasted time. I use my bull-riding skills more than I use my math skills."

"I bet you use math skills."

He smiled crookedly. "Yes. I'm great at counting to eight."

"All the way to eight?" She smiled back. "I knew you were smart back then. I listened to you answer questions when you deigned to come to class. It bothered me that you didn't take advantage of your education."

"Yes. I recall a time when you made that clear."

She shrugged unrepentantly. "Somebody had to do it."

"I disagree."

"Come on…it made you all the more determined to succeed."

He leaned closer, even though he told himself not to.

There was something about her wide green eyes and full lips that made him forget his own pep talks. "Are you trying to take credit for my success?"

"I figure I'm due at least fifty percent of your winnings…and don't worry about the math. I'll do it."

"Comforting to know."

She picked up her beer and drank, watching him over the rim. He would have given up a win at that moment to know what she was thinking, because he knew what he was thinking, and what he didn't want to be thinking. Moisture glistened on her lower lip when she lowered the bottle and Austin's groin tightened as he thought about licking it off.

He blew out a breath and reached for his beer. When in doubt, take refuge in alcohol.

They said no to dessert. Austin paid for the meal. Kristen told him she was keeping track of what she owed him, and, to keep the peace, he'd simply nodded as if he fully intended to accept payment in the future.

They crossed the lobby and were almost to the elevators when a loud voice called, "You! Asshole!"

Austin turned to see a very drunk Braden Crawford heading across the lobby toward him with murder in his eye.

"Do you know him?" Kristen asked, putting a hand on his arm.

"Yeah." Austin took hold of her arm. "Stay here." He let go and started toward Braden. A security guy was also heading toward the young bull rider.

"You stole my sponsor!" Braden stumbled as he spoke and Austin grabbed his arm and yanked him toward the door.

"We're good here," he called to the security guy.

"Not until you're off the property, you're not."

"Going," Austin said, wrapping his arm around Braden's neck in a choke hold and moving toward the door. Kristen started after them, but he was in no position to control Braden and convince Kristen all was well, so he just kept walking.

"Like fuck we're going," Braden choked out close to his ear. Austin moved his head so he didn't get bit. Drunk bull riders could be unpredictable creatures. The security guy followed them until Austin dragged Braden to the public sidewalk twenty yards away from the hotel.

"See you again and I'm calling the police."

"Officer…?"

Austin glanced over his shoulder to see Kristen catch up with the security man and start talking earnestly to him, then he continued down the sidewalk with the flailing and struggling bull rider, glad that he had a few inches and several pounds on the wiry kid.

When they were a safe distance away, he let go, then ducked the roundhouse punch the kid threw. "Stop, or I'll have to get serious," he growled.

"Took my fucking job!" Braden backed up a few steps, his face screwed up in an angry grimace. "I was going to make it back to the top. I'm not staying in the minors forever!"

"Yeah. I know." Braden was also drinking too much and getting himself into too much trouble. His sponsor had taken notice. Cut him loose. Offered Austin the sponsorship, which he had accepted today.

He looked over his shoulder, saw the security guy heading back to the hotel and Kristen still standing at the edge of the parking lot.

"Go back to the room," he called to her. "I'll be up shortly."

"No."

Austin rolled his eyes at the stubbornly protective note in her voice. "Please go. Braden and I will talk and then I'll be up." Braden launched himself at him while he was talking, but Austin easily wrangled him back into a hold. The guy was so drunk that he could barely keep his feet under him.

"I got this," he said as Braden grunted. "Go."

"I'll wait in the lobby," she said stubbornly.

"Thank you."

"The security man said that he's calling the cops if you don't get clear of the property."

"Noted."

Kristen headed across the parking lot, her shoes making soft noises on the asphalt, and Austin turned back to Braden, who'd stopped struggling. Austin loosened his hold and then jerked his head toward the park across the wide street.

"Come on, man. We're going to talk in a place where we won't be arrested."

KRISTEN TURNED WHEN she reached the hotel and saw Austin guiding the drunk man across the street. She watched for several minutes after they sat down, and when no violence ensued, she went into the lobby and took a seat in one of the cream-colored leather chairs. Once settled, she looked over her shoulder toward the park. Austin and Braden were just visible from where she sat and it appeared that Austin had the situation under control. He'd had it under control from the moment the man had called him an asshole.

People skills. Maybe she should be taking notes.

The security man walked past her and she smiled at him. He nodded back before casting a frowning look through the glass doors toward where Austin and the other guy were deep in conversation, across the street from hotel property.

"Are you waiting for them?" the security man asked.

"For one of them."

The man gave her a stern look. "I don't know that either of them are welcome back."

Kristen channeled the cool confidence/arrogance that had protected her so well and caused her so much trouble. "The man *I'm* waiting for was accosted at dinner. He's an American Extreme Bull Rider, with national sponsors, and he has an image to maintain. I promise you that he's just trying to get this guy under control so that he can take him to wherever he's staying."

The guard blinked at her, as if debating the truthfulness of her story, so Kristen let her expression ice over just a little more. "You can check the registration. Austin Harding. Bull rider."

The guard gave a small cough, making her wonder if he was a bull-riding fan. "That other guy had better not be staying *here*."

"I'm certain he's not."

Kristen's phone dinged as the security man gave her one last hard look, for good measure apparently, then continued on his way. She pulled the phone out of her purse. Austin.

'Go to the room. I'm going to be a while.'

Kristen went to look out the tall glass windows that flanked the door. Both men were looking her way, as if fully expecting her to check on them. With a sigh, she turned toward the lobby and crossed to the elevator. Fine. She'd go to the room and worry there. Although, it appeared that Austin still had the situation well under control.

She hated the unknown. Hated unresolved situations.

Hated being told what to do.

She let herself into the room, wondering how long Austin was going to be.

Not long, it turned out. She'd barely gotten into bed when the door opened and Austin walked around the partition and turned on his bedside light. She pushed herself upright. "No black eye, I see."

He blew out a breath and sat on his bed. "Nope."

"Where's…" She hesitated to call the guy his friend.

"In his room a couple of floors down."

"How'd you get him past security?"

"Never underestimate a bull rider." She frowned at his non-answer and he said, "Got lucky. Slipped by while he was busy dealing with someone else."

"You depend on luck a lot, don't you?"

"Have to. Skill can only get you so far. Circumstance and luck do the rest."

She didn't argue the fact. "If you don't mind telling me, what was the deal between you two? How did you steal his job?"

Austin started prying off his boots. "He got busted down to the minor league tour. Started drinking too much. His sponsor took notice."

"And he blamed you?"

"I got his sponsorship today."

"Seems like he's responsible for that."

"He's young. Only nineteen."

Kristen's mouth flattened. "All the same."

"Bull riding is a tough gig."

"I noticed."

Austin stood, his hands resting loosely on his buckle. He shook his head, then headed for the bathroom as Kristen burrowed deeper into her blankets. A few minutes later he came back out and she listened as he undressed, turned off the light and then slid into bed.

"Is he going to be okay?" she asked in a low voice.

"No telling." There was a flatness to his voice. Resignation to things he couldn't change, but wanted to.

Kristen pulled the blanket around her a little tighter. Austin's life, his chosen profession, was fraught with uncertainty. How on earth did he deal with it, day in and day out? But deal he did.

"Are you okay?" she asked in a low voice.

"Fine."

He didn't sound fine.

"Maybe you can talk to him when he's sober."

"Don't think that'll do a lot of good."

It was hell wanting to help someone and not be able to do it. She wanted to help Austin; Austin wanted to help his fellow bull rider.

She rolled over, trying not to think about the guy lying few short feet away from her, staring up at the dark ceiling. She shifted positions a few minutes later and tried to force herself to relax.

What would happen if she made a bold move, got into his bed?

According to him, he'd kick her out again to save them from doing something they'd regret.

No...to save her. She was certain of that. It wasn't as if

she was going to break Austin Harding's heart.

She balled her pillow up under her head even though she felt more like putting it *over* her head. Then maybe she wouldn't be able to smell the warm masculine scent drifting her way, hear him moving in his bed.

"Kris?"

She froze. "Yes?" Her voice was barely audible.

"Are *you* okay?"

She almost said no, she wasn't okay, but she wasn't going to pile something else on his plate. If he'd wanted to sleep with her, he'd be in her bed right now.

"Yes. I'm fine." If one didn't count tension, frustration at not being able to help, and gut-level desire to feel a hard body pressed against her own.

"Then, please…for the love of all that's holy…go to sleep."

Chapter Nine

"NEW SPONSOR! THAT'S great! Now you need to land a documentary film, like your brother."

Austin gripped the phone a little tighter. His dad had called early and Austin decided it was time to answer. "I don't want to be the subject of a documentary, Dad."

His brother, Ty, hadn't been that wild about it in the beginning, but it had worked out for him.

"You've got to strike while the iron's hot."

"Yeah." Austin pressed a hand against his forehead, wondering for the umpteenth time what his stage-mom father was going to do when both of his kids were out of the business and he could no longer be a vicarious champion.

"I know some people—"

"Dad…"

"Okay. I'll keep my mouth shut. For now. But if you change your mind…"

"I'll let you know. I've got to start working out now. Could you put Mom on?"

"Sure thing."

"Thanks, Dad. I appreciate the support."

After talking to his mom, he ended the call and stuffed his workout clothing into a small grip bag. He'd do his physical therapy in the gym today. Kristen had been politely friendly, yet somehow distant, this morning before going to breakfast without him when his dad called, thus setting the tone for the remainder of their time together.

He liked her.

More than he should, but their time together was limited. She was working to break free, as she'd called it, and to be more flexible—hell, she'd practically propositioned him—but she was still Kristen Alexander. Overachiever with a mission in life, and she'd be back at that mission after making peace with her family. She'd probably end up being vice president of a bank or something, and he would... He didn't know. He had money in the bank and no idea what he was going to do for a career once he was done riding bulls.

Something would shake out, and until then, he'd focus on winning this tour.

The other bull riders would be drifting into town today and tomorrow. There were sponsor parties and pre-functions to attend, and he and a couple other riders had a signing at a big western store on Friday before the prelims. If all went well in the prelims, he'd ride again on Saturday and on the following day he'd drive Kristen to Marietta.

Two weeks later he'd be in Portland, once again traveling alone. He really should hook up with someone and share a ride, since it didn't look like his usual travel partner, who, along with Braden, had been demoted to the minors, was going to be back on the main tour any time soon.

Or maybe he'd continue his solo act. It felt comfortable.

Although he was beginning to think that comfort was overrated. He couldn't say it was easy having Kristen sharing a room with him—but it was interesting. And he was having a hard time shoving her out of his brain when he needed to focus on other things.

He was going to have to work harder at that—for both their sakes.

KRISTEN WAS BEGINNING to think that Austin was avoiding her. She'd left the room that morning when he'd taken the call from his father, and found it empty when she came back forty minutes later. It was still empty when she stopped by after spending a couple hours taking in the sights, and when she returned later that afternoon, she found a note propped against the television saying that he was out with some bull riders who'd just got into town. Possibly the same crew he'd been with at the Silver Bow.

"Be back late," the note read. "Charge your dinner to the room."

The last bit sounded like an order. Austin might be a take-charge kind of guy, but that didn't mean he needed to take charge of her, or direct her activities when he wasn't there. She'd pay for dinner herself, thank you very much.

Kristen took the elevator down to the lobby and spent some time perusing the magazines and books in the lobby gift shop before buying a box of microwave popcorn and a Diet Coke. She'd just put her charge card back in her purse when someone behind her said, "Excuse me."

She turned to see the young bull rider who had called Austin an asshole the previous evening standing behind her. He pulled his hat off, his face going red as he said, "I was, uh, hoping to see you before I left. I want to apologize for the scene I caused."

"Thank you." She didn't know what else to say, other than maybe he shouldn't drink so much.

He gave her a jerky nod, then abruptly turned and walked away, clamping his hat back on his head as he left the gift shop.

What would it be like to be nineteen and have your dream on the skids? Bull riders did not have long careers for obvious reasons. Some guys lasted longer than others, competing into their thirties, but for the most part, that didn't happen.

It hadn't happened to Braden.

Which made her wonder what was going to happen to Austin. He was twenty-six—old in this game. He didn't seem all that concerned about life after bull riding. She'd been guilty of the opposite—she'd spent so much time plotting and planning the future that she hadn't enjoyed the moment she was in. The only mistake she'd made was in thinking her job was secure and not socking away enough money for the future. And again, Austin was the opposite. He had money socked away, but she couldn't help believing that he probably would have been just as satisfied with his life if he didn't.

She headed for the elevators, glad that the young bull rider had gone the opposite direction—hopefully steering clear of the security guy. The door to the elevator that had taken her and Austin on the wild ride the day before opened and Kristen stepped back to let the people move past her.

"Hey," one of them said coming to a stop next to her. "I know you."

Her stomach fell as she met the eyes of the Brazilian bull rider who'd been with Austin that night at the Silver Bow. The one who'd taken such great interest in her costume. The upper part of it anyway.

She felt the frozen deer-in-the-headlight feeling coming on and did her best to stave it off with a weak smile. "Yes. I remember."

"That was a helluva trick you pulled on Austin," the bull rider said, pushing his hat back. His dark eyes were dancing with amusement. "He fell for it."

"For a while anyway," the other guy, whom Kristen also recognized from the casino, said. "He figured it out pretty fast, but damn, girl. Good one."

Kristen found that her smile was becoming more genuine

at the bull riders' earnest congratulations. "I regretted it afterward."

"Austin needs shit like that." The Brazilian extended a hand. "Gustavo Santos. Gus."

The other bull rider also leaned in for a handshake. "Josh McIntosh."

"Kristen Alexander."

"Salt Lake City is a long way from Reno," Gus said.

"I'm on my way home to Montana."

He gestured with his head in the direction of the bar. "You want to join us for a quick drink?"

Her first instinct, as always, was to say no and escape, but she was trying to do things differently, so why not? A quick drink. It wasn't like her microwave popcorn would go bad, and she was curious about these guys. More bad boys of the cowboy world. "Sure."

"We're not keeping you from anything?" Josh asked as they started across the lobby.

"Not a thing."

"Pretty girl like you?" Gus asked going into such exaggerated lady's-man mode that Kristen had to laugh. She was still smiling when they navigated around a marble column and ran smack into Austin, who was also heading for the bar.

The look on his face when he saw her with his friends was almost comical, and then his expression cleared and his jaw muscles tightened.

"Austin, look—we found your friend. The one with the

rattlesnake," Gus said as if Austin would need a hint as to who she was.

"Yeah." He shifted his attention to Kristen. "I was up in the room looking for you a few minutes ago." He was wearing a freshly ironed and starched shirt, so yes, he probably had been.

"I was down here." She held up the plastic bag. "Dinner."

"I thought you were going to charge dinner to the room. Like a real dinner."

"Changed my mind."

The two bull riders exchanged looks, then burst out laughing. "You two?"

"I'm taking her home," Austin said, his voice clearly indicating that he wasn't in the mood to take any crap off them.

Josh reached out and patted Austin on the shoulder. "I guess you guys made up."

"Guess it's none of your business," Austin countered pleasantly, but there was an edge to his voice.

"We were going to have a quick drink before your function," Kristen said.

He turned back to her and there was something in his expression that she couldn't quite read. "I was trying to find you to see if you wanted to go to the function."

"Am I invited?"

"You will be."

Well, wasn't that a surprise? Kristen took in the bull riders' polished boots, starched shirts, shiny trophy buckles, then calmly met Austin's gaze. "I don't have anything to wear. I packed light, remember."

"Maybe we could go upstairs and look."

"Or you could have a drink with us," Gustavo said with a crooked grin. The guy was definitely not shy.

Kristen looked at the trio of bull riders and shook her head. Part of her wanted to go have her damned drink and the other part wanted to go to the room and have a few things out with Austin.

"Maybe another time," she said to Gus, who winced as if he'd been hit.

"You bet," Josh said.

"Maybe we can hook up tomorrow," Gus suggested. "After the prelims. You can have a drink with the winner."

"I'll give her your number," Austin said, taking Kristen's elbow in a light grasp and steering her toward the elevators.

"What was that about?" Kristen asked through her teeth as they walked back across the lobby. She took a sideways step when they stopped so that his hand dropped away.

"We can talk in the room."

They caught the elevator they'd kissed in, but this time it took them straight to their floor with no side trips. Good. She had things to say to him and didn't need to be distracted. As soon as they got to the room, Austin went to her closet and opened the door. Kristen closed it again and his gaze jerked up in surprise.

"Do you really want me to go to this function? Or were you just trying to pry me loose from your friends?"

"I know my friends," he said darkly.

"That isn't an answer." She drew in a breath and asked the question that had been bouncing around in her mind since Austin interrupted her trip to the bar. "What business is it of yours who I hang with?"

"I didn't think you needed to end up in Gustavo's bed."

She gave a short laugh. *Really?* "And maybe that's not your call."

His gaze dropped to the carpet and he ran a hand over the back of his neck before looking back up at her. "I know it's not my call."

"Thank you," she said with exaggerated politeness.

"But be warned—Gustavo will treat you like any buckle bunny on the tour."

"Maybe that's what I'm looking for."

His eyes went dark. "You sure about that?"

She took a step forward and tilted her chin up to meet his gaze. Anger made it so much easier to say what she thought. It always had. "I'm sure that I can do what I want, see who I want. You aren't in charge of my...scars."

"You don't even know him."

"Well, the guy I *know* isn't interested."

"Kris...have you ever had a one-night stand?"

Her gaze slid down to his mouth, which was set in a flat

line as he waited for her answer. "What do you think?"

"I think no."

There was an intensity in his expression that made it impossible to look away.

"Don't start with Gus."

He stepped back and shoved a hand through his hair before giving her an accusing look. "I'm trying to do the right thing here."

"I wasn't thinking along those lines either." *Not much anyway.* "But something changed. *Somebody* kissed me. Got me thinking. Got all those high school fantasies roused up again." One corner of her mouth tightened ruefully. "Good ones, too."

He sat down on her bed, his jaw muscles tightening as he stared past her, his expression intense. Too intense.

Needing to regroup, Kristen turned to the closet, pulled the door open. "Do you still want me to go to this function with you?"

The door swung shut, startling her, since she hadn't heard Austin move. She turned to find him only inches away from her, his jaw muscles still so tight that she could see the pulse beating there.

"Do you want a one-night stand, Kris?"

"I…" The answer died on her lips. Any doubts about whether he was attracted to her evaporated in the sizzling heat of his gaze. She swallowed, managed to force a single word out. "Yes."

He brought his hand up and lightly stroked his fingers down the side of her face, sending a shiver through her.

"Last chance for sanity."

"Not taking it."

"You're sure?" His voice was low, almost a growl. Rather than answer, Kristen touched his face, holding his gaze as she ran her thumb across his firm lower lip.

He caught her hand, brought her knuckles to his lips. "Lead the way, Kris."

Her heartbeat skipped as she realized what he was saying. He wanted her to take charge. To prove that he wasn't taking advantage. The old insecurities started to rise, but she made a Herculean effort to put them aside.

If he wanted her to lead, she'd lead.

Without a word, she took his face between her palms and slowly pulled his mouth down to hers. But instead of kissing him, she teased his mouth, stroking his upper lip lightly with her tongue, nipping his lower lip. Doing her best to show him she could take charge. Austin stilled, met her gaze. She lifted her eyebrows.

He gave her a so-it's-going-to-be-like-that look, then pulled her against him, claiming her mouth. So much for her taking control. But she'd make her point and then there was no more thought of insecurity. Only Austin challenging her to let go. To forget everything except the sensual fire he was stoking with his lips, his tongue, his fingers. He slid his hands down over her ass, pressing her against his hard length before traveling back up her sides, brushing over her breasts, making her swallow first a gasp, then a groan as his thumbs brushed over her nipples through too many layers of fabric.

There was no more ice princess. In her place was a woman whose insides were blazing.

She sucked a breath between her teeth as his lips traveled down the side of her neck to the sensitive hollow there, before moving back up to her mouth again. Her nipples strained against her bra as he cupped her breasts, teased them through her cotton dress, her bra. There was simply too much fabric between them. She needed to feel his hands on her skin, not on her clothing.

She turned and moved her hair aside, offering him the zipper of her dress. He took hold without a word, smoothly drawing it down to her lower back. She shrugged her shoulders and the dress skimmed down over her hips and fell to the floor. Stepping out of the pooled fabric she turned to him. There was nothing between them now except for expensive lace, cotton and denim.

Austin addressed the cotton, popping the snaps of his shirt one by one, exposing his chest, his rock-hard abs. The scars on his pecs and the big one curving around his side.

"Someday you'll have to tell me about all these scars." As soon as she spoke, she regretted it. One-night stand, remember? Except that she didn't believe this was going to be a one-night thing…not when they had more nights together before heading home.

"Which one do you want to know about?"

She touched the small one on his pec, first with her fingers, then with her lips. His skin was salty, which made her want to trail her tongue along the contours of his body, tasting as she went. Oh yeah. She was a salt girl.

"I was young. Riding a bull whose horns hadn't been blunted. Stupid."

She continued her exploration of his scars, of the hard planes of his chest and abs, without further questions. Time for that later. When her hands reached the top of his jeans, she looked up at him. "Any scars down here?"

His chin dipped lower, watching as she undid the trophy buckle on his belt. His flat stomach contracted as she dipped her fingers beneath the waistband of his jeans and undid the top button.

"Feel free to explore."

She stepped back and gestured at his feet. "Boots, Austin."

He sat on the bed and pulled off his boots. Then he stood and unzipped his jeans, pushed them down over his muscular thighs, bringing his boxers with them. When he straightened, his erection bobbed impressively. Kristen looked first at his hard-on, then met his gaze and held it as she reached out and took his cock in her hand, running her hand over the heavy length of it.

And then, she stepped forward, hands now on his chest, forcing him back until his knees hit the bed and he sat. That was when she lowered herself down between his knees and slowly drew him into her mouth. Felt a small rush of power.

Austin's head dropped back and his eyes closed as she sucked, teased, tasted, until he abruptly pushed himself upright. His breath was ragged as he said, "Yeah. That'll do for now."

She slowly got to her feet, dragged her gaze from his swollen cock to his face. He made a circular gesture with his finger. "Turn around."

When she did, he pushed aside her hair and undid the clasp of her bra, then tucked his thumbs into the sides of her panties and rolled them down past her thighs. Kristen's breath hitched as the silk slid down her legs, then she inhaled sharply, when he lightly nipped the cheek of her ass.

If she was wet before, she was drowning now.

He put his hands on her waist, turned her around and pulled her down beside him on the bed, where his hard body pressed against hers. But what she thought was going to be a quick coupling, turned out to be a long, slow exploration of her body—every part of her body. He worked his way to her most vulnerable area, and she gave a tiny whimper as his tongue flicked over her sensitive clit. One more touch like that and she'd be done for.

Austin must have read the warning signs, because he abandoned his mission and pulled himself back up alongside of her, stroking her hair back from her face, and dropping a quick kiss on her lips before getting out of bed and walking to his bag. A moment later he was back.

He settled a knee between her thighs, a hand near her head as he positioned himself over her, the blunt tip of his cock pressed against her. She had the strong feeling that he was giving her one last chance to back out, but there was no going back. He waited until her taut muscles relaxed before he started pushing himself into her. He was less than halfway in when she followed instinct and arched against him, hard, burying him all the way inside of her.

"Is that what you wanted?" He murmured the question close to her ear.

"Yes." She couldn't think of anything that had ever felt better than Austin inside of her.

He lifted his hips, pulled almost all the way out of her, then slowly drove into her.

"Like that," she murmured.

His cock throbbed inside of her and then he began moving inside her with a steady rhythm. Slow, but not too slow. Then fast, but not too fast. Touching that magical spot some people said didn't exist. It did. And it was sending wicked sensations through her every time the end of his cock hit it.

Oh. No.

"Don't…"

"What?" He stopped instantly, his hand coming up to her cheek, his eyes dark with concern.

She pressed against him. "Don't let me come too soon."

He let out a breath, shook his head, then started again

with a serious motion, his strokes long and deep. She felt the climax building again, fought against it. It was too soon, way too soon.

"*Austin…*"

He didn't slow down. He kept moving, his rhythm increasing, his body beating into hers. Her control was slipping…and then it was gone.

She cried out against his shoulder as her body exploded. She arched against him and then came down to earth in a thousand small pieces. Austin gave one final deep stroke before his head dropped and he half collapsed, taking care not to drop all his weight onto her.

As if she cared.

She smoothed the damp hair away from his forehead, bringing her cheek to rest against the side of his head. She closed her eyes, let out a low breath as his hand came up to cup her breast.

"I can't remember the last time I felt this good," she murmured.

"I'm doing okay on this end, too." He ran a hand over her back in a slow soothing motion.

She let herself relax against him, wishing they could simply go to sleep, but he had the function to go to. "What happens now?"

"What do you mean?"

"I don't want things to get weird, you know…after we get back to Marietta."

He raised an eyelid to look down at her. "When reality takes over?"

"Exactly."

"They won't get weird." He sounded like he fully believed what he said, and that helped Kristen believe as well. "We'll enjoy this time while we have it, then real life will kick in and we'll go back to being friends. The important thing is that we know that going in. Know what we want. Know what we expect."

"Sounds good." It also sounded like a free pass to do what she'd never dared do before—enjoy life in the here and now, with no big plans for the future.

He rolled over onto his side so that they were face to face. "Tell me something."

"What?"

"How'd you get that scar on your upper arm?"

"My scar?" She twisted her arm so that she could see the J-shaped white mark. The accident had happened such a long time ago that she rarely thought about her scar—especially since she couldn't see it.

"It's how I knew it was really you in the casino that night."

She made a face at him as she let her arm drop back onto the bed. "Taken down by my past."

"I was almost convinced that it wasn't you until I saw it."

And maybe, considering all that had happened between them, that was a good thing. "I was fencing with my cousins on the MCC ranch one summer. The wire they were pulling snapped and whipped back. I was lucky it only hit my arm."

"Shit."

"I know."

He rolled her over onto her back and gave her a long, lingering kiss. "I need to go."

"You do," she agreed.

"I want you to come with me."

"I honestly have nothing suitable for a western event."

"I don't trust Gustavo not to slip away and come calling. We'll find something."

Kristen nipped his lower lip, smiling when he gently returned the favor. "No worries there. One bull rider is plenty. I don't need two."

Chapter Ten

AUSTIN KEPT A loose hold of Kristen's fingers when he finally led her out of the hotel suite where the American Extreme Bull Riders meet and greet was still in full swing. They'd done the social thing—met sponsors and deep-pocketed fans. Answered questions, drank good liquor. And for the entire hour and a half that they were there, all Austin could think about was getting Kristen back to the hotel room.

He would let her lead this relationship, because she had the most at stake. If they got back to the room and she decided that another sexually charged romp was not what she was looking for, he could deal. But on the other hand, if she wanted a lot of good sex with a guy she could trust, he was her man.

From the way she wrapped herself around him as soon as the hotel room door closed behind them, he deduced that she hadn't changed her mind.

And he was damned glad of it.

This time when they made love, it was hard and fast. A sprint to the finish, ending in a satisfying tie.

He waited until they caught their breath before asking, "What are your plans for the future?" He brushed a lazy finger down the side of her face. "Because I know you have a plan."

She sighed and stared up at the ceiling. "My plan is to make a plan."

"So nothing definite."

"Which isn't easy for me." She rolled onto her side. "I've always had a direction, an immediate goal, a long-term goal. They built one on top of the other and it was all so damned smooth."

"You'd never considered the possibility of being laid off?"

"Call me naïve, but no. I'd worked hard and expected to be rewarded. And then I wasn't, so now I have to figure out how to get back on track."

"Do you want to get back onto the same track?" he asked slowly.

"What do you mean?"

He dropped an arm over her, pulling her closer. "I mean that the plan you made for your life when you were sixteen, or eighteen, or twenty might not be right for you now. Sometimes you have to change."

She angled her head so she could see him better. "I could say the same thing to you."

She had a point. He'd been following the same vision since high school. "My plan is still working."

"But for how long?"

"Until I stop winning enough money to stay on the tour…or until I incur a debilitating injury."

Her muscles tightened beneath his palm. "That's crazy."

"That's bull riding."

"You have no intention of quitting while you're ahead?"

"What's the point of being ahead, if you're going to quit?"

"Having the use of all your many body parts?"

"I can't quit, Kristen."

She rolled onto her side, cupping her palm against his cheek. "Why?"

"Hard to explain."

"Try?"

"Bull riding is…" How could he articulate the deep need to do the impossible? To challenge and be challenged? He let out a breath. "Give me a little time on this."

"If you come up with an answer, let me know. Because I'm beyond curious." She stroked her hand along his side, down to the hollow of his hip, where it came to rest.

"Don't be disappointed if you never get the answer, because some things can't be put into words."

She bit her lip, as if fighting a smile. "I'm aware."

He slid his hand over her gorgeous ass, pulling her that much closer as his dick started to swell. "Are you?"

A nip on his lip answered his question. Communication without words. His favorite kind. He rolled her over, found her lips and lost himself in a slow exploration of her mouth as his fingers zeroed in on her warm, wet center.

She pressed against his hand as his finger slipped inside of her, and all thoughts of explaining his love of bull riding evaporated from his brain.

KRISTEN COULD SUM up the focus of her life in her Salt Lake City hotel room in three simple words: sex with Austin.

And if she wanted to expand her summary to four words, it would be: more sex with Austin.

She was pleasantly tired and a little sore and beyond satisfied with her breaking free adventure—but now that she was seated in the VIP section of the American Extreme Bull Riders venue, waiting for smoke and fire to announce the beginning of the performance, reality was starting to filter its way into her insular break-free world. She was going home tomorrow. Back to real life and all its complications.

Living a freeform life, drifting, sounded like fun, but it wasn't realistic to someone like her who didn't have a lot of money in the bank. Who didn't ride bulls for a living.

Austin wouldn't be able to ride bulls forever.

And he didn't know what he wanted to do when his career was over. Kristen smiled a little. That should bother her more than it did, because he was not being sensible, but Austin seemed to have a way of landing on his feet. And he was as driven as she was. He'd figure something out.

The house lights dimmed and the music started, pounding out a primitive beat, energizing the audience as the bull riders strode through the smoke and took their places along the flaming line. Austin was facing away from her, feet spread, hands on his buckle in a classic bull rider stance. She now recognized names from the party where she'd met the other riders—Casey, Cody, Gage. When Austin's name was called, she felt a well of pride and possessiveness. Her bull rider.

The music hit a crescendo as the bull riders started back toward the chutes. Austin looked her way as he followed T.J. Casey out of the arena, and even though she was certain he couldn't actually see her, he touched the brim of his hat before disappearing through the gate next to the chutes.

She came close to lifting her hand in response. And it was suddenly kind of scary to feel this connected to a guy whom, logic told her, could only be a fleeting part of her life.

The price of breaking free, having her adventure.

She could deal with the situation—it just might not be as easy as she'd first assumed.

THERE WAS NOTHING better than being on top of the game, and that was exactly how Austin felt as he straddled the rails over Prime Time. He set a foot on the bull's back, letting him know that the routine had begun. Prime Time barely acknowledged him as he then settled in place near the flank strap and started working the rope.

Two wins in a row. That was the goal. Prime Time was an unpredictable bucker, changing up his modus operandi each time he came out of the chute, but Austin was okay with that. He had a talent for reading subtle cues, noting the tells.

He did a quick prep, wanting to get on with the ride. Once the tail of the rope was folded into place, he tucked his chin, patted the rail and nodded. The next thing he knew he and three-quarter tons of bull were high in the air just outside of the chute.

Prime Time's front legs pounded back down to earth. Seven seconds left.

The subtle roll of muscle under his left thigh and the spin began, into his hand.

Six...Five...Four...

His chest jerked and his shoulders snapped back as the spin abruptly ended and Prime Time changed directions with a twisting ass over ears maneuver that caught him off guard, pulled him away from his hand.

Shit.

Muscles burning, he pushed deep into his feet, fought like hell to keep from going down, but gravity had a mad hold on him.

Three...Two...

He struggled, teeth gritted, sheer determination keeping

him in contact with the bull as about a thousand G's pulled on his wrist—

The horn blew as he felt the air between his ass and the bull.

The earth met him in a teeth-jarring crash. Dirt stung his face, and then his entire upper body lifted as the bull stepped on his calf, his hoof sliding off his boot. His face hit the dirt again as pain seared through his lower leg.

Son of a bitch.

He squeezed his eyes shut, the dirt in his lashes stinging his eyes. There was a thud next to him, not loud enough to be the bull, and he raised his head to see the bull fighter peering down at him. Immediately he started pushing up to his feet. A hand slid under his arm and he made it all the way up to vertical.

One limping step and the crowd roared. The score came over the loudspeaker, but he didn't catch it. Eighty something. Enough for the finals?

Another step and his leg felt as if it was going to explode right then and there.

He wouldn't give in to the pain. Another step. Another.

Out the gate and on past the guys who clapped him on the shoulder, toward the medical room at the other end of the long concrete hallway. A medic who'd been at the chutes caught up with him, put a hand under his elbow, helping ease the burden on his sore leg.

"How bad?"

"You tell me. I just hope you don't have to cut the boot off. It's new."

SO THIS WAS *what it felt like to have one's stomach turned inside out—and have it stay that way.*

Austin had walked out of the arena after the bull had trod on his leg, but it had been all Kristen had been able to do to stay in her seat during the remainder of the event. She'd tried to bluff her way to the contestants' area, only to be stopped by security, who were taxed with the job of keeping the groupies at bay until the bull riders appeared to sign autographs. She went back to her seat not knowing whether Austin was behind the chutes supporting his friends, or if he was in an ambulance, heading for the nearest medical center.

This is what he does. This is what all these guys do.

And, judging by Braden Crawford, it was devastating to them when they could no longer ride bulls competitively. A different breed, these bull riders. She couldn't imagine embracing the unknown on a weekly basis, taking a chance at ending her career each and every time she went to work.

Kind of made getting laid off look boring.

After the performance ended and Kelly Kincaid, a bull rider who had just made his way up from the minors into the American Extreme Bull Riders Tour, was named the winner,

Kristen headed for the exit where she was supposed to meet Austin. This time the security pass worked and she made her way along a concrete corridor. Austin came out of a set of metal double doors as she approached, dressed in gray sweatpants and a long-sleeved T-shirt, his leg strapped into a protective boot.

"Precautionary," he told her. "To stabilize it until I get to the hotel."

"Then you can take it off?"

"I'm going to." He gave her a smile that didn't quite hit his eyes. "How're you doing?"

"Me?" He was asking about her after he'd been stomped on by a bull?

"Yeah."

Her first instinct was to put on her cool unperturbed face and pretend she was doing just fine with his near-death experience. Her second was to tell him that it had scared the crap out of her. She chose the middle ground. "Working my way through it."

"I can't drive. They gave me a painkiller. It's starting to take hold."

Kristen took the keys from him, and then reached for the bag he was carrying.

"I'm not helpless."

"Do you have to do the autograph thing?" Kristen asked as if he hadn't spoken.

"Not while I'm under the influence."

"Let's go home." A bittersweet feeling settled over her as they walked to the parking lot. After tonight, there was no more 'home' for the two of them. Home was a pretend place. A hotel room where they could hide from the world and real life.

She was going to miss it. Miss him.

How had she come to feel a deep connection to this guy with whom she had so little in common?

Opposites attract.

Yes, but attraction wasn't the problem. It never had been. It was living at opposite ends of the personal and professional risk spectrums that created issues…but after tonight, she wondered if she was as far on the safe end of the spectrum as she'd once believed. It had terrified her to see Austin get hurt, but while sitting next to the other bull riders' families, she'd heard equal parts analysis, cheering and praying. They'd worked out a system to handle the stress, and if she needed to, so could she—and it didn't need to apply only to bull riding.

KRISTEN NAVIGATED THE post-event traffic like a pro and got them back to the hotel, where they surrendered the truck to a valet. Austin beat Kristen to his bag and stubbornly hefted it out of the back seat before opening the door and stepping out onto the asphalt with his good leg. Pain shot through him as his left leg hit the ground, but he could bear weight, which was a good sign. The doc hadn't been able to tell him much, and he'd been ordered to get an X-ray in Marietta to see exactly what the damage was.

Austin wasn't keen to do that. Didn't want a potential fracture to get in the way of finishing the season. If he could walk…well, he was okay.

Kristen was all business as she ushered him to the room, and even though the pain meds were making him foggy, he found it a turn-on. He did love it when his ice princess showed up. She unlocked the door and stepped back so that he could enter first. Once the door was closed, she eased past him to place his bag on the desk and to drop her purse beside it.

He sat on the edge of the bed and started unfastening the pseudo-cast on his injured leg while Kristen disappeared into the bathroom. She came out a short time later wearing the T-shirt and plaid shorts that had been her sleep outfit until two nights ago.

He'd call that a signal. She flipped back the covers of her bed and sat on the edge.

"Need any help with anything?"

"Yeah. My boot." As in singular.

"Sure." She came to the side of the bed where he sat and gingerly eased the orphaned Tony Lama off his foot. "What happened to the other one?"

"Cut down the side and sitting in the trash can at the

arena."

"That's too bad." She helped him peel off the sock then grimaced and he took a look. Yep. Black as hell.

"Is it broken?"

"I don't think so."

"What about your ankle?"

"I don't think so."

"Are you sure?"

He gave her a look. "The problem seems to be the place where the bull stepped on my leg."

He sounded snarky, so he drew in a breath. Closed his eyes and tried to center. This was why he was no fan of pain meds. They made him cranky. Edgy. Obnoxious. Not his normal state of being. When he opened his eyes again, he found Kristen smiling at him, as if she knew exactly what was going on with him. She shook her head and went back to her bed.

As soon as he'd stripped to his boxers, he got into bed, then decided what the hell. He liked sleeping commando, and just because Kristen was back in pajamas, it didn't mean he had to follow suit. He got his shorts down over his injured leg, kicked them to the end of the bed, then settled in.

And there he lay.

He had two weeks to get back into fighting shape before the tour started again in Portland. If he had to be injured, this was the time. Yes, it was.

He might not make it to the exhibition he'd agreed to in Pendleton, Oregon, during the hiatus, but he would make Portland, Spokane, Nampa... He'd make all the events right up to Championships. He'd ridden with worse injuries, but the problem was that compensating for one injury could lead to another.

So be it.

Part of the game.

He shifted his hips, tried to get more comfortable.

"Shouldn't you elevate that foot?" Kristen's voice came through the darkness.

"Probably." Definitely. Why hadn't he done that?

Foggy brain.

"Kris?"

"What?"

"Why are you over there?"

He glanced over his shoulder at her, saw that she was propped up on one elbow, staring at him through the semi-darkness. "So I don't hurt you." She spoke as if it were patently obvious why she was a good six feet away from where he wanted her to be.

He closed his eyes, drew in a breath. "I think you should come over here and risk hurting me."

"Austin..."

"It'll help me sleep."

She didn't answer, but a long moment later, he heard her push back the covers and get out of her bed. "I'm keeping my T-shirt and shorts on."

"Fine."

"And elevating your foot."

"I'd appreciate that." He rolled onto his back.

She retrieved a sofa cushion and pulled back the sheet to gently settle his foot on it. Then she got into bed and settled about two feet away from him. He reached out to pull her closer to him.

"Just don't jar anything and I'll be fine."

"I don't know how bull riders' wives handle this," she murmured as she snuggled closer to him. She curved her hands over his shoulder, one on top of the other, and settled her head on his pillow. Their lower bodies were separated by several inches.

"I guess they adapt to circumstances."

"Guess so." Her breath feathered over him as she spoke and even through the pain meds had half-numbed him, it felt good. "I'm afraid to move," she said.

"I like having you here. It's our last night... I didn't want to spend it alone.

Chapter Eleven

AUSTIN WOULD HAVE driven the seven hours north from Salt Lake City to Marietta if Kristen had let him. She wasn't about to allow that, so when he headed to the driver's side of the truck the next morning, she bluntly told him that he was the passenger. He didn't argue about the driving, but he refused to take another pain pill. Kristen wasn't going to force any kind of a drug on anyone, but she hated seeing him hurting.

Hated seeing *anyone* hurting, she qualified, doing her best to convince herself that what she felt for Austin was the same as what she'd feel for any injured person; but it wasn't. How could it be, after what they'd shared over the past several days?

She would never be the same. That was a given. Her time with Austin had continued what losing her job had started— hammering home the lesson that when life got messy, she didn't need to religiously follow the carved-in-stone path that she'd chosen at the age of eighteen—or to feel bad when she couldn't follow the path. Side trips were legal—and sometimes they were forced upon you. She'd served drinks in costume and hitched a ride with a bull rider. She'd survived and she'd grown. And she'd had awesome sex.

Glancing sideways, she saw that Austin's eyes were closed and his features relaxed. *Finally.* Every time she'd woken the night before, he'd been staring at the ceiling. He'd fallen asleep just before daylight, so she'd slipped out of bed and started dressing, hoping to slip out for coffee without disturbing him, but he woke up before she could leave. And, somehow, she'd resisted the temptation to crawl back into bed with him.

She was going to miss him, but the thing about side trips was that they had to end before they went sour. She and Austin were no longer in their insulated Salt Lake City hotel-room world. Things would be different in Marietta, and, as she saw it, she and Austin were ending on the perfect note at the perfect time.

He slept for most of the trip home, occasionally shifting and screwing his face up in pain, but not waking. These bull riders were a tough lot. Kristen kept her focus on the road, except when she looked at him, drinking her fill while she could. Austin pushed himself upright with a painful grimace when she pulled up in front of the house she owned with her sister. Her haven until she found another job.

"We're here," he said, blinking.

"We are." At the place where they would go their separate ways. She smiled a little. "Part of me doesn't want to return to reality."

"It's always that way after a vacation." He met her eyes. "I'm not sure what to say now." She solved the problem by leaning over the console and sliding her hand around the back of his neck, pulling herself close enough to kiss him. Hard. He answered her kiss, his hand coming up to cup her cheek.

When she leaned back, he smiled and her heart did an odd double beat. "I know what to say…thank you for helping me break free for a little while."

"Any time." His smile held a mixture of acceptance and regret. "Good luck with the job search."

The screen door of her house banged and Kristen looked over her shoulder to see Whitney coming down the porch steps.

"Thank you." There was so much more she could say— all the many things she'd silently philosophized about as she drove, but Kristen wasn't going to try to put anything into words. They understood each other and that was enough. "Are you sure you can drive to the ranch?"

He snorted dismissively and reached for his door handle. Question answered.

Austin limped to the driver's side of the truck as Kristen got out. "Hey, stranger," he said as Whitney reached the gate.

"Austin." She lifted her eyebrows at his pronounced limp. "How're you doing?"

"No complaints."

"Will we see you at FlintWorks before you head out again?"

He rubbed a hand over the back of his neck. "More likely I'll be at Grey's…no offense."

"Yeah. I know. You're a traditionalist."

"Old habits die hard." Austin got into the truck, gave the twins one last smile, then put the vehicle in gear and pulled away from the curb.

And that's that. Kristen let out a breath, doing her best to ignore the heavy, melancholy feeling that settled over her as she turned to her sister, who was regarding her curiously.

"I'm gearing up to face the music. How are the folks?"

"The folks are looking forward to seeing you. Dad got called into the ER to cover for Dr. Gallagher, so you won't see him until tomorrow morning." Whitney shot a look toward Austin's truck as it disappeared around the corner. "So…you two?"

Whitney was never one to be sidetracked for long, but Kristen gave it a stab. "Let me deal with Mom and Dad and then we can have a nice long talk."

And maybe after dealing with her parents, it would easier to talk about Austin. In a few days, she'd have her bearings, feel more herself. Be back in control. And maybe, if she was lucky, the memories of their time in Salt Lake City would start to fade.

AUSTIN DROVE SOUTH on Highway 89 to the Forty-Six Ranch, the place his brother called home. The truck seemed empty without Kristen, but he figured the feeling would pass. They're shared some intense moments over the past several days, and he could be forgiven for suffering from withdrawals. Never in his wildest thoughts would he have guessed that he and Kris could bring out so much in one another.

She was right—it *was* hard to ease back into real life. But ease he must. He had a leg to heal and a tour to win.

When he parked next to the barn, Les Connor, his sister-in-law's grandfather, came out the door and approached the truck. "You'll be staying in the house," he announced in a no-nonsense voice.

"Good to know."

"Can you walk that far?"

Austin narrowed his eyes at the older man. "What makes you think I can't?"

"Eighteen-hundred pounds of bull treading upon you."

"Watched the tour?"

"Every televised event."

That would be all of them.

"Are you on painkillers?" Les asked with a lift of his thick gray eyebrows.

"Nope."

He jerked his head toward the house. "Then let's go have a beer while we wait for Ty and Shelby to get back from checking the fence."

"I could use one." Austin slid out of the truck, taking care as he stepped down to the ground. He'd put on the stabilizing boot again for good measure, but as long as he was careful, he could support some weight on the leg, which meant he probably wasn't going to have that X-ray.

When Ty and Shelby got home, he kissed his sister-in-law, man-hugged his brother and then settled in on the porch for the questioning. It was unusually warm for the last day in April, so Ty gave Austin and Les their second beers of the day, and set his own beer and a bottled water on the table between the two unoccupied chairs. He disappeared into the house, then came back a few seconds later. "Shelby will join us in a few minutes. She said we could commence brother talk without her."

Austin smiled and opened his beer.

"How's Dad handling the injury?"

"Didn't answer when he called." Austin only answered every second or third call. His dad didn't hold a grudge about it. He just kept trying.

"Probably wise."

"He's used to it." Austin was much better than his brother had been at handling their father's tendency to try to manage them. He'd learned by watching. "I'll call him in a couple of days. I did send him a text telling him I was fine and not to worry."

"Did he try to get you a documentary?" Austin gave his

brother a speaking look and Ty laughed. "It's not that bad, actually."

"And the chances of two guys in one family landing documentaries…"

Ty laughed again. "I know. But you can't blame the old man for trying."

"Or me for dodging him when he gets set on this kind of stuff."

"I hear ya."

Austin gave his brother a frown. He was a different guy since hooking up with Shelby. Not only happier…he was mellower. And he now seemed fine about his career being over.

Shelby came out onto the porch then, her hand lingering over her midsection in a way that caught Austin's attention before she sat down next to Ty, who handed her the water. Once again her hand settled on her belly and Austin sent his brother a look.

Ty gave a solemn nod, then put his fingers to his lips.

Son of a bitch. He was going to be an uncle. No wonder Ty was okay with his career ending. He was about to embark on another. Austin gave a quick nod and focused back on his beer. He should have suspected when Ty got Shelby bottled mineral water without asking her what she wanted to drink.

Austin looked up again and gestured toward Les with his chin and Ty shook his head.

Okay. Just the three of them were in on the secret.

He wanted to tell someone. He wanted to tell Kristen.

Not going to happen. Over. Done. Fun while it lasted.

It was going to take a few days for his inner self to get it through his inner head, but facts were facts. He'd enjoyed his time with Kristen, enjoyed watching the layers peel away as she shed inhibitions—even if her newfound confidence had given him pause every now and again. But their time of sharing secrets was over.

"How long are you staying?" Shelby asked.

"Just a couple days. I'm appearing at a benefit in Pendleton and I thought I might get a house close to the beach for a couple days after that. Enjoy some peace and quiet before the event." A few days alone might help him get his shit together. Then, when he came back through Marietta, he could look Kristen up. Take her to dinner. By that time, she'd be back on the job search and he'd be a pleasant memory. In other words, they would have both come to their senses.

"Nothing like quiet time to heal." Shelby had hung around rough stock riders long enough to know exactly what he was doing.

"Exactly." He grinned at Les. "I know I'll get put to work if I stay here."

"That's a fact," Les agreed easily.

He wouldn't have minded working if he wasn't hurt. He liked work. In that regard, he and Kristen were alike. They were both driven—just in different directions.

"Do you know if you have a fracture?" Shelby asked.

"I prefer not to know." His leg was damned sore, but he was riding regardless.

"Stay out of hospitals," Les muttered. His hatred of hospitals was legendary.

"I'll do my best," Austin said with a laugh. Although his chosen profession sometimes made that a difficult promise to keep.

"Check the leg out," Shelby said. Ty nodded in agreement and Austin gave a noncommittal shrug. He'd have it checked out when he thought he needed to. Right now it was only slowing him down on the ground. He could still push weight down through it, as he would when he rode. It hurt like a son of a bitch, but what was new there?

"How'd it go?"

Whitney poured Kristen a tall glass of ice tea as soon as she walked in the kitchen door. She waited for her sister to take a drink before asking, "Did they understand?"

'They' being their parents. Less than an hour after arriving in Marietta, Kristen had walked the two blocks to her parents' house to set the record straight about her life. They had been more stunned by her secret keeping than by her layoff. After she explained her logic—how she'd thought she could land something fast, but time had slipped by more quickly than she'd anticipated—her dad had kind of gotten it. Her mom was still working on the secret part. Working hard on it, in fact.

"She was embarrassed to get fired," her father had said to her mother, as if Kristen wasn't sitting right there. Embarrassed.

"Laid off, Dad."

"Whatever."

They'd talked for almost an hour, and after Kristen laid out the stark reality of her situation—lots of applications in lots of places, but no real responses—her parents had gone into protection mode, offering solutions, possible places of employment. But they weren't happy and her mother kept studying her, as if half expecting her to say, "Surprise, just kidding. I never lied to you."

"Well?" Whitney prompted.

"Did *you* understand?" Kristen asked as she stirred sugar into her tea. She needed a jolt of something. Sugar would have to do, since Whitney didn't have any booze in the house.

"Of course not...until I cooled down and recalled that you're competitive as hell *and* a perfectionist."

"I am not."

"Argumentative, too."

"Funny." Kristen leaned back in her chair and took in the cheery kitchen with its sunny yellow walls and cherry motifs on the white curtains and dish towels. Her twin loved color and retro style. Kristen had given her carte blanche to do whatever she wanted with the house they'd inherited from their grandmother. The result was a colorful, fun interior that made her feel like smiling. Most of the time. Right now she was dealing with the sting of parental disappointment—disappointment she could have prevented by being upfront.

"What did you think would have happened if you'd told us when you lost your job?"

Kristen shrugged. "I…thought you guys would be disappointed in me."

"Well, it wasn't like the earth would stop spinning."

"It felt like it." Stupid, but it had. She'd been hard on herself for a long, long time…and that was going to stop. This time she'd temper her self-discipline and drive with some self-care.

Whitney gave her head a shake. "Remember how I played T-ball and you didn't?"

Kristen frowned at her, wondering what had caused her to dredge up that particular memory. "Because I had trouble hitting the ball—"

"And running."

Kristen snorted. "So it took me a while to learn to bend my arms. Big deal."

"Anyway," Whitney continued, "I was tearing up the ball diamond, and you weren't, and Mom used to say—"

"That's okay. Kristy is good at school."

"Exactly."

Kristen let out a sigh. She didn't need a degree in psychology to understand that that simple statement, spoken like a mantra during sporting events, had sown a seed. Kristy *would* be good at school, and her job, come hell or high water.

Whitney gave her a weary smile. "I know it wasn't purposeful on the folks' part—heaven help me, when I have a kid, I'll probably screw him up every which way from Sunday—but I think celebrating our 'differences' might have just scarred us a little."

"It wasn't them. It was me. I let old habits run my life instead of taking a long hard look."

Kristen reached for the ice tea pitcher and poured a refill. "I guess scars make us tough."

Whitney turned in her chair, then held up her leg, showing the cleat marks in her calf from her days playing softball. "I'm real tough."

"I'm tougher than I was."

Whitney put her foot back on the floor. "Yeah? What made you tough? Getting fired?"

"Laid off. Yes, that, and serving drinks in a casino bar. And—"

She was about to say, in the most casual of ways, 'traveling with Austin,' when Whitney interrupted her. "You served drinks?"

"For six whole days, and yes, I should have told you. I'm telling you now."

"How'd that go?"

"I wore a saloon girl costume."

Whitney's eyes looked like they were about to pop out of her head. "You wouldn't wear Halloween costumes!"

"I made up for it. Believe me. It was so low cut I thought my boobs were going to pop out at any second. And I wore fishnet stockings that felt like cheese graters on my feet."

"You were that desperate?"

"Yep."

"Did you get decent tips?"

"I sucked at getting tips. And I got fired."

Whitney laughed, but it wasn't in any way hurtful. "I'm not surprised. No offense."

"None taken." Kristen gave a small snort of laughter. "I was not a good waitress. But I met Austin while I was working and he agreed to give me a ride home." That sounded suitably casual. Just a matter of meeting a hometown guy and bumming a ride when she needed it. Or so she thought.

"Before or after you got fired."

"After."

"So you had to find him?"

"It wasn't hard. He was at the events center. I walked in and asked him for a ride. He agreed."

"So what's going on with the two of you?"

Since she'd lied about losing her job, she had to take care not to push the truth too hard. "We're friends." That was true.

"Friends."

"Yes."

"If you say so…but that was one helluva lip-lock I witnessed."

Kristen hadn't realized that her sister had seen them kissing. After all, the windows were tinted. "Whit…"

"However…" her sister raised her hands as if surrendering "…it isn't any of my business…unless you want to talk."

"I don't." Not yet anyway. She wanted to keep her thoughts, her feelings, her memories close. At least until she got her rather jumbled emotions sorted out into their neat little boxes again.

"Fine. Even though you promised."

Kristen frowned at her twin. How could she adequately explain Austin and breaking free and her short sortie into the land of here-and-now with no thought to the future? She couldn't. "Let's get back to me disappointing the family."

Whitney took a sip of her ice tea. "I'm done. However, I'm available if you ever want to talk."

"Thank you."

"And the little parlor is free if you want to set it up as your war room while you tackle the job market."

"I appreciate that." Her sister knew her well, although, oddly, she didn't feel that keen about tackling the job market—a side effect of her trip that she hadn't anticipated.

Whitney lifted her glass and gave a wry smile. "I thought

you might."

AUSTIN COULDN'T HELP around the Forty-Six as much as he wanted with a bad leg and sore shoulder, but he did what he was able to do, most of it on horseback. He rode fence and made rudimentary repairs prior to turning out the cattle, spending the better part of four days covering the property looking for winter damage. He told himself that the time alone on horseback was better than time alone on a beach. He loved the ocean, but understood that Ty was trying to get Shelby to take it easy, which was why he volunteered for fencing duty.

He thought about Kristen a lot. Wondered about her. Kept his distance. That was the agreement.

After the fences were finished, he and his brother moved the cattle while Shelby took Les to a medical appointment. When they got back, Austin had a message on his phone from an old rodeo friend turned educator, asking if he could speak at a small Oregon high school on his way to the Portland event.

"What kind of speaking?" Ty asked after Austin hung up.

"Like giving a speech to the high school kids about pursuing non-traditional careers."

"Non-traditional."

"That's what Teller called it."

Ty pulled two beers out of the fridge, then turned toward Austin, who'd just set his phone on the kitchen table. "You, who barely *showed up* for high school, are now going to *address* a high school? As a role model?"

"They don't know I didn't show up much." Austin took the beer his brother handed him and gave a small salute.

"That's ridiculous."

"No more ridiculous than Teller McKay settling down and becoming a school guidance counselor."

"Point taken."

Teller had been the most daring rough stock rider either of them had ever met up with. He rode bulls and broncs—often in the same rodeo—until his body broke down at the ripe old age of twenty-three. Then he'd gone to college and became a guidance counselor. Both Ty and Austin had expressed concern about what he might guide students to do career-wise—*forget college…have you considered rodeo?*—however, he seemed to have found his niche. In fact, he took his job very seriously and now he wanted Austin to speak on the matter of setting non-traditional goals, to inspire the kids who didn't fit into neat academic boxes.

"What in the hell should I say to these kids?" The enormity of what he'd just agreed to was starting to reveal itself.

Ty shrugged. "You accepted the gig."

"Have you ever tried to say no to Teller?"

"It isn't like he'd hunt you down…" Ty's voice trailed

off and he and Austin exchanged pointed looks. "All right. He might."

"I'll probably have to make notecards."

"Yeah. That sounds good."

"How'd you remember what to say in your documentary?"

"I just said whatever and they edited. There wasn't a script."

"Huh." Austin tapped the table with his fingers. If he could ride a bull, he could make a speech. Even if it scared the shit out of him.

"So you're leaving early?"

"A day at most."

"I'll tell Les so that he can get your revised chore list ready."

"Thanks," Austin said dryly. "I'm sure it'll help keep me limber."

Chapter Twelve

"I SAW AUSTIN today."

Kristen's heart did a double beat as Whitney sauntered into her job-searching war room, but her voice sounded gratifyingly normal as she said, "I thought he'd be in Oregon by now."

"He's not. He and his sister-in-law stopped by Flint-Works." Whitney held up her glass in a salute.

Kristen shrugged, hoping the stress of trying to look unconcerned wasn't making her face pink—because the truth was that memories of Austin weren't fading as quickly as she'd hoped. "Well, he'll probably be leaving any day."

"Probably." Whitney was watching her closely and it was getting annoying.

"What?" Kristen asked in a flat voice.

Whitney made a frustrated gesture. "Nothing. I guess."

Kristen dropped her head back. She could keep stonewalling, or she could come clean and stop the searching looks. "No big secret, Whit. Austin and I got together and now we're going our separate ways."

"It's really none of my business."

Kristen drilled her sister with a hard look. "No kidding."

"But after the secret unemployment, I'm worried about you, okay?"

"Allowed."

"So if you broke up, then that was a goodbye kiss?"

"We didn't break up because we were never together. Well, we were, but with an understanding."

"No-strings-attached sex?" Whitney sounded slightly incredulous.

"More than sex. Hard to explain. Let's just say...we understand each other and what we needed from one another and what's realistic for the future."

"No-strings-attached sex."

"We were more than fuck buddies." The words blurted out and then Kristen snapped her mouth shut. Where had that come from?

She cleared her throat, but before she could speak, Whitney said, "It's hard to explain. I get it." She grimaced at the sticky-note-covered wall Kristen had created in the course of her job search. "You had your fun and now you're back."

"That does kind of sum it up."

"You and Austin...what happens now?"

"I don't know. I've never done anything like this. We're supposed to be friends."

"Who are out of contact."

"Probably for the best while we settle back into our niches." Because giving up sex with Austin hadn't been the easiest thing she'd ever done. And she missed telling him things that she probably wouldn't tell anyone else. Sex partner. Confidante. Not a fuck buddy.

Whitney still had an odd look on her face, so Kristen changed the subject. "I have a job interview."

A wide smile brightened her twin's face. "In Montana?"

"In Reno, believe it or not. One of my contacts came through. I have an interview." She explained the situation as she and Whitney went to the kitchen, where Whitney pulled a bottle of white wine from the fridge. She poured two glasses without asking Kristen if she wanted one. Some things were simply understood.

"Sounds like he wants to hire you." Indeed, her former colleague who'd gone to work for another company had sounded very interested in hiring her.

"I hope so. It would solve some problems." Money, security. Things like that. And now that she knew what it was like to *not* have a job, she'd be double vigilant about what was going on with the company—as she should have been before. The odd thing was that she didn't feel like dancing in the streets at the prospect of going back to the place she'd called home for a number of years. She loved Reno, she wanted a job, so what was the deal?

"How long do you think this process will take? Before you know?"

"No telling." That was the hell of it. "It depends on how

I stack up against the other candidates. What my references say about me. A lot of things play into it."

"Want to wait tables?"

"Funny. Ha. Ha."

Whitney sipped her wine, watching Kristen over the rim of her glass. "No. I don't mean it as a joke. We need a sub at FlintWorks. Just until our college girl, Macy, arrives in two weeks. You'd earn a little cash, and it would keep you busy."

"You're serious? Knowing my history? Six days waiting tables, then fired?"

"If it doesn't work out—"

Kristen's eyes went wide. "What? You'd fire me?"

Whitney shrugged. "I'd pretty much have to."

Kristen gave a sniff. "Well, I wouldn't mind the cash." And she wasn't a total newb at serving drinks…plus, she'd be fully clothed.

"You'd have to work the crappy shifts."

"Don't sugarcoat it."

Whitney laughed. "Want to come down to FlintWorks and meet my boss tomorrow?"

Kristen pretended to consider for a moment, even though she'd already made up her mind. She could conduct her job search around FlintWorks shifts. It would do her good to get out. More than that, she wanted to get out, which was very out of character. Her time with Austin honestly had done her some good. That was the part of their relationship that she was going to focus on…not the twinges of regret about never having sex with him again. Never laughing about stupid stuff in the wee hours of the morning.

"Kris?"

Her attention snapped back to her twin. "Yes. Definitely. I'm all about meeting your boss."

"Just don't embarrass me."

"What would it feel like to have your twin embarrass you?" Kristen asked.

Whitney peeled a sticky note with a phone number off the clipboard sitting on the counter between them and stuck it onto Kristen's forehead. "No. Idea."

WAITING TABLES AT FlintWorks was very different than serving drinks at the Silver Bow. For one thing, her body was fully covered. When Kristen looked down, she saw the bright blue FlintWorks staff shirt, rather than her breasts threatening to escape lace-edged red satin. And she wore running shoes instead of fishnets and bootie shoes. Her feet were happy. She was happy.

After breaking in on Sunday afternoon, she had a crazy patchwork schedule. An afternoon followed by an evening, followed by a lunch shift, followed by another evening. No rhyme or reason, because she was filling in here and there as needed, but she didn't mind. It wasn't as if she had anything else on her agenda, other than the continued job search and her prospective interview in Reno.

Her cousins, Shane and Cody Marvell, had stopped by toward the end of her first shift and invited her to the ranch to help with the spring fencing repairs. She declined their kind offer, but enjoyed catching up with her rowdy cousins after she'd clocked out.

"You're into numbers, right?" Shane's question jerked her back to the present. "Accounting and stuff like that?"

"Yes."

Shane dropped an arm over the back of his chair in a casual gesture. "Can you help me with my taxes?"

Kristen's jaw dropped. "You know taxes are due on April 15th, right?"

Her cousin gave her a charming smile. "I filed for an extension. I want to write off some of my rodeo expenses, but I don't want to pay penalties later. A lady friend of mine barrel races, and she just got nailed. Wasn't pretty."

"I'm not a tax person per se...but I'll see what I can do."

"Maybe you could help me, too," Cody said.

"You haven't filed either?"

Cody sent his brother a look. "No. I'm thinking about starting a business in addition to the ranch. I need some advice."

Kristen propped a hand on her hip, narrowed her eyes. "You guys aren't making up stuff to help your unemployed cousin, are you?" She wasn't about to be the family charity.

Cody and Shane shook their heads in unison.

"Our ranch accountant is swamped," Cody said. "We'll pay whatever the going rate is."

"The family rate is free."

"Then we'll find someone else," Shane said easily.

"You guys are awful."

"Yeah," Cody said. "We are. And we're paying you."

On Monday, Kristen learned the ropes of lunch service, which was almost as exhausting as a busy night at the Silver Bow. She'd just finished bussing a table, and was about to take a break when she noticed Whitney signaling her to the bar. She crossed the room with her loaded tray, then nearly dropped it when she spotted Austin half perched on a barstool. Her heart slammed against her ribs as she met his oh-so-blue eyes, then let her gaze slip down to his half-smiling gorgeous mouth.

He looked…better than she remembered.

How could that be, when he'd been pretty damned perfect in her head?

"Hey," she said with what she hoped looked like an easy smile. Her heart wasn't supposed to start hammering like this. It simply was not.

This was the moment when they kicked off their new relationship—their casually friendly relationship that was manageable and realistic. This was not the moment for her hormones to hopefully whisper, "May we have more, please?"

No. No more. Not doable. You're an accountant. He's a

bull rider. No middle ground. Remember?

Yes. That was the thing to focus on—no middle ground. And she would focus hard.

She set her tray on the bar as her insides tumbled with anticipation of something she wasn't going to get. *Take it easy—it's going to take time for kinetic memory to fade.* And pheromonal memory. He smelled so damned good, and the scent reminded her of long nights in tangled sheets.

"Just came to say goodbye."

Whitney headed to the far end of the bar and started polishing glasses. Kristen shot her a look, then said to Austin. "Are you going to order something?"

"Nope."

"You only came to say goodbye?"

His expression softened. "Seemed like the thing to do."

Kristen felt the same. She'd wanted to say goodbye, wish him luck out on the road. "Let me drop off this tray and I'll walk you to your truck." She hoped she made it. She hadn't expected just seeing him again to have this kind of effect on her—to make her knees feel all rubbery and her chest tight.

"Sure."

She took care of the tray and clocked out for her break. Austin was waiting by the door when she came out of the staff room. Lindsey, the other server, gave her a thumbs-up and Kristen somehow refrained from rolling her eyes. Yes, Austin was thumbs-up worthy, but Lindsey had misread the situation between them.

"You're moving better," she said as they stepped outside and started toward Austin's truck.

"Drugged out of my head."

Her eyes went wide before she realized he was kidding. Okay. Good. Tension was now officially eased.

"The leg is feeling better." He stopped close to his truck, cupping the keys in one hand. "I'm surprised to see you back in the service industry."

"It's different here." She fought a smile. Lost. It felt good to talk to him. "I have an interview. A Reno company."

He gave a small laugh. "Reno. Of course."

"It's a company I had targeted from the beginning."

"Good luck with that." Austin folded his arms over his chest. "I'm...uh...giving an inspirational speech at a high school in a couple days."

"Really?" She tried not to look surprised.

"Yep. I'm going to talk about taking a non-traditional path to success."

"You're the poster child for that."

"I am."

Kristen smiled as an awkward silence settled over them. She wanted to move, but she was afraid to move.

Austin shifted his weight. "Well, I just wanted to say goodbye."

She nodded, her gaze traveling over him, stirring memories and causing yet another swell of heat to warm her body from the inside out. She swallowed. "I appreciate it."

"Good luck with the job interview."

"Thanks."

Austin dropped his chin to his chest, then raised it again. Their gazes met. Held for one heart-stopping electric moment.

This isn't wise.

Austin reached for her, almost as if he couldn't help himself, and a second later her arms were around his neck; her mouth was on his. He grew hard against her stomach as he ran a hand over her hip, cupped her ass and pressed her against him.

A car pulled into the far end of the lot and they broke apart, putting a good two feet of gravel between them. Austin shoved his thumbs into his belt loops and Kristen folded her arms over her chest, but their gazes held. He wanted her. She wanted him.

Not good.

Kristen cleared her throat. Her face—make that her entire body—felt like it was on fire. "That was...unexpected."

"Was it?" He swallowed after he spoke.

"I'd convinced myself it was."

"We're going to have to work harder."

"Yes." She meant it. "Like maybe not see each other."

"Do we need to go that far?"

"We might."

When they'd been in Salt Lake City, she'd convinced herself that after they'd returned to Marietta, to their everyday lives, their perceived closeness would be revealed for what it was—something ethereal, created in a false environment. Something that couldn't stand up to reality. They would be friends, but not confidants and lovers. That had been just a quick side trip. Her adventure.

"Don't think too hard about this."

Kristen frowned at him, disturbed that he knew exactly what she was doing. "Yeah. Right." How was she not supposed to think about this?

He tipped her chin up. "We'll get this under control."

"Probably, because there's a good chance we won't be bumping into one another all that often."

"Which is why you don't need to think too hard." He spoke in a low voice that made her insides tumble again.

"Good luck on the rides."

He gave her a cocky smile, but it didn't reach his eyes, which remained fixed on her face. "Always."

She could barely suppress the urge to lean closer, to kiss him again, which was crazy. And what was crazier still was that part of her wanted to climb into his truck and take off with him—to return to their fantasyland.

Never in her life had she felt an impulse like this.

The guy was like a drug.

"I have to go, Austin."

"Me, too." He reached down and took her hand, pressed a kiss into the palm, then closed her fingers over it.

"Give it time. Things will mellow out. We'll be okay."

She clenched her fingers around her tingling palm. "Yes," she said in a determined voice. "We will."

Chapter Thirteen

AUSTIN'S LEG ACHED whenever he put weight on it, which meant that it ached full-time, so he sat in a chair while signing autographs after the Portland event. He considered himself fortunate that the extent of his injuries thus far in the season were the usual aches and pains in the shoulders, elbows, knees and wrist, and a possible fracture of his fibula. He signed his last autograph, smiled at the little girl who took it from him as if it were something precious. "I'm going to ride bulls when I get bigger," she said.

Her mother's smile went tight, as if terrified that her daughter would do just that.

"My advice is to start small," Austin said. "With sheep."

"I'm already doing that."

"Wear all the safety equipment. No matter what. Only uncool people refuse to wear helmets and vests."

"But what about Gustavo? He doesn't wear a helmet."

Austin smiled. "Like I said…"

The night had gone well. He hadn't won the big money, but he hadn't gotten any more busted up than he already was, and he'd picked up a travel partner the day before. Kelly

Kincaid, who'd come out of nowhere to win Salt Lake, was struggling with finances and there was some issue with his truck that he hadn't gone into too deeply. Whatever the deal was, Austin was glad for the company. Driving alone for hours gave him too much time to think. He normally didn't mind being alone and thinking, but lately his thoughts seemed to edge more toward Kristen and less toward mental preparation for the next event.

Nothing wrong with that…except that, like the kiss in the FlintWorks parking lot, he hadn't seen this coming. Hadn't expected to have Kristen haunting his thoughts more and more, rather than less as time passed.

He'd assumed that after he'd been on the road for a day or two, he'd ease back into his old routine. Training, doing appearances, focusing on the next event. Hanging with his friends. He hadn't thought he'd be fighting the urge to call Kristen and touch base, hear her voice. What good would that do him?

He met Kelly in the changing room and the two of them walked to his truck.

"I appreciate this," he said for the tenth or eleventh time.

"Glad to have company," Austin replied, just to change up his usual 'not a problem' response.

Kelly gave a nod. He was normally a talkative guy— Austin had hung with him a few years before, when he'd spent time in the minors—but, despite the win in Salt Lake and his high finish tonight, he didn't have a lot to say.

Austin was good with that.

Nothing wrong with a little quiet.

KRISTEN HAD JUST pulled her car into the driveway after a late shift at FlintWorks when her phone rang and her heart jumped. Late-night calls were never good…especially when Austin's name appeared on the screen and it was possible that he was calling to tell her he'd been injured. She hadn't yet had a chance to find video of Austin's ride, or search for results of the Portland AEBR event, so she had no idea how the finals had turned out.

"Hello?"

Please, be okay.

"Hey." His voice rolled over her and she relaxed against the seat. He was all right. "I, uh, just felt like checking in."

"How was your ride?"

"Awesome."

She gave a low laugh in spite of herself. "Any part of you get twisted, crushed, or bent?"

"Yes."

She laughed again. "Any chance you could expand on your answer?"

"You don't want to know tiny details." She did, but she wasn't going to push. His tone shifted, became more candid. "I came in third. Had good rides. Nothing got hurt any worse than before."

"Good to hear." He'd made some money and would be pushing on to the next stop—Spokane, Washington.

"Did you hear back on the interview?"

"Well, I interviewed via the internet, and now I'm waiting. No idea when I'll hear whether I made the cut to the next level. How'd the high school talk go?"

"They listened to me." He sounded surprised, although she wasn't—who wouldn't listen to a guy who risked his life in a big way every time he went to work?

He told her about his speech, how he'd prepared and used notecards, because he thought he was supposed to, until they got into the way of what he wanted to say.

"That happens," Kristen said, thinking that this call felt too intimate for the type of relationship they both wanted, but she wasn't about to end it.

"Not to me. I skipped speech class as often as possible. Took the D."

"Why am I not surprised?" He gave a low laugh, and she realized that she wanted to hear him laugh again. Enough. "I should go."

End this call. Get back to reality.

"Yeah. Me, too. I don't know when I'll be able to call again."

"That's okay." It was supposed to be, anyway.

After Austin said goodbye, Kristen went into the empty house, changed into her sleeping T-shirt, then lay in bed watching his rides. She knew he'd done well, but that didn't keep her heart out of her throat as she watched eight long seconds of action. Twice.

In both prelims and finals he'd ridden until the horn blew. Both times he dismounted and made it to the gate unscathed, but he was limping more than before after his final ride. That damned leg injury. Had he had it looked at?

She'd bet not.

She replayed the videos. It was obvious he was doing what he loved. Grit and determination were evident in every practiced move he made as he prepared for the rides. The confidence in the quick nod before the gate opened and the bovine Kraken was released. The stunning skill he showed as the bull gyrated, twisted, bucked and reared.

He raised his hand in victory after both rides. Despite the limp, he carried himself like a champion as he left the arena.

He was a champion. Doing what he loved. Pursuing a dream that could be crushed at any moment.

That took guts.

Kristen put the phone aside and closed her eyes, picturing Austin striding across the arena, ignoring his limp, focusing on his victory. The guy had panache.

The guy made her ache.

AUSTIN'S WIN IN Spokane, following his painful third-place

finish in Portland, came at a price.

Riveter had given Austin one hell of a ride, then sealed the deal by hooking him before he could get to his feet, tossing him sideways. Austin landed on his bad leg, which once again turned bluish black, and this time the sports medicine team told him to stop fucking around and have the leg X-rayed. If it hadn't been fractured before, it certainly was now.

Less than an hour later, Austin had his answer—a fracture of the fibula, mid-shaft, thank goodness, which was the best of all possible breaks. He was good to go for the rest of the season, as long as he protected the leg. Of course, riding bulls made that an iffy proposition, but he'd do his best.

Kelly suffered a dislocated elbow and a wrenched ankle during the prelims, so the trip to Nampa was slow and easy. They arrived the day before the meet and greet and took it easy, hanging out in the hotel spa, putting their battered bodies on display for anyone who cared to glance their way. Both wore AEBR ball caps as they let the spa jets work their sore muscles, and it didn't take long for word to spread that there were honest to goodness bull riders in the spa. The kids showed up first, followed closely by women, some young, some older, all kind of interested in what a body looked like that went through hell every week.

Kelly focused on the water, not making eye contact, even when a couple of women slipped into the opposite side of the spa and smiled at the two bull riders.

As they'd driven from Portland to Spokane last week, Kelly had finally let out his story in fits and starts. He was married and his wife had left him mid-tour because she couldn't handle the stress of his career. Austin had extrapolated that last part, but it made sense. The wife was gone. Kelly's truck was gone. Kelly was in a perpetually shitty mood. He'd experienced the same thing more than once, only without the rings on the fingers. For that he was grateful.

"I'm heading back to my room," Kelly said as another woman eased into the spa. He stood up, water sheeting off him, oblivious to disappointed looks sent his way.

"Yeah. I'm coming, too." Austin smiled at the ladies, then followed his friend. He was glad to escape. He had tapes to watch, and he wanted to stretch while his muscles were loose from the hot water and jets…and since hooking up with Kristen, he hadn't had much of an eye for the women. She'd kind of ruined him in that regard. As it was, he had to stop himself from reaching for the phone and contacting her a couple dozen times a day.

The important thing was that he *was* stopping himself, thus allowing Kristen to move on without worrying about him.

Yep. Moving on.

He got into the elevator with Kelly and they rode up to the ninth floor where they went their separate ways. Kelly was pinching pennies, but had sprung for a decent room in

Nampa and Austin suspected it was for his lady, just in case she decided to join him.

For Kelly's sake, Austin hoped that happened. And if it didn't—well it'd be a long, silent ride to Cheyenne.

LESS THAN TWO weeks after Austin's call from Portland, Kristen was on the road to Reno for her interview—the interview that might have saved her from the consequences of her half-baked scheme had it happened four or five weeks ago.

But you would have missed out on your Austin time had that happened.

Maybe things really did happen for a reason.

She adjusted her sunglasses as she topped a hill and starting driving into the setting sun. Seventy more miles. The freeway stretched before her as she traveled through broad alkaline valleys bordered by naked mountain ranges on both sides. She could drive from Reno to Marietta and back three times for the cost of one last-minute plane ticket, and frankly, she needed the time alone.

Her brief stint at FlintWorks had ended two days ago with the arrival of Macy Crandall, the girl interning at the microbrewery as part of her course of study. Having made enough in tips in a little less than two weeks to finance the Reno trip and cover her student loans, Kristen now understood why Whitney was happy tending bar. She was doing all right.

Kristen was doing all right, too. She'd sent off Shane's taxes yesterday morning on her way out of town—and it was good thing he'd hired her, because his accounting system was trouble waiting to happen, or rather, an IRS penalty waiting to happen. In addition to straightening him out, she'd advised Cody on the pros and cons of sole proprietorships, LLCs and corporations, and helped two of her mother's friends learn to use a digital accounting program. Shane and Cody had insisted on paying her, but she'd drawn the line at her mother's friends, who had eventually settled for giving her homemade raspberry jam and a plate of scones. Kristen loved jam and scones, so that story had a happy ending, too.

Her story with Austin…she wasn't sure how that one was ending—but she sensed it was indeed ending. He hadn't called her after Spokane, even though he'd won. That was telling and Kristen told herself she was good with it.

She should be, anyway, because it was part of her original plan. They were easing back into their own worlds. Older. Wiser.

Lonelier.

She missed him.

When Kristen drove out of the canyon into Sparks, the first thing that struck her was the traffic. She wasn't arriving at the best time of day, but still…how could she have forgotten about the traffic in such a short period of time?

She got off the freeway as quickly as possible and took the side streets to Lynn's place, where she was claiming the sofa. Tomorrow she interviewed, then immediately got back in her borrowed car and started the drive to Montana. Once there, she'd finish her cousin Cody's business plan. Spend some quality time with her parents and sister. Enjoy her time in Marietta.

She liked living in Reno. But she also liked being closer to her parents and her sister and had been thinking about the benefits of living in Marietta more and more. What better time to make a move than when she didn't have a job?

You have an interview.

She did…and she also knew she wouldn't be heartbroken if she didn't make the final cut. She told herself it had nothing to do with Marietta being the closest thing Austin had to a home base.

She was, of course, lying to herself.

PROTECTING A FRACTURED leg was no easy task in Austin's line of work, but he did what he could, and the medical team did what they could, taping and supporting. His shoulder was also taped, as were both wrists. The rides were starting to take their tolls, but he was more than halfway through the tour and still ambulatory, which was more than some of the guys could say.

His partner for the evening was Stillwater, a former bull of the year, who showed no signs of mellowing as time passed. In the chute, he worked against the clock, trying to get the bull prepped before his time ran out. Every time he thought he had it, Stillwater reared, or worse yet, dropped his front end, making it nigh on impossible to get situated. He was sweating hard when he finally got set and gave the nod.

As soon as the gate opened, Stillwater set about doing his job—and he did it better than Austin did his. Three seconds into the ride, he ate dirt. A lot of dirt. His head was ringing when he jumped to his feet and ran for the rails with the half-skipping gait he'd developed to keep as much weight as possible off his fracture. Stillwater ran by, gave him an obligatory headshake, then disappeared out the gate.

Austin sucked in a long breath. An early out for him, but Kelly was up next and the guy rode with teeth-gritted determination. If he didn't have his wife, at least he'd have a win.

When the end of the performance came around, Kelly was no longer in the high-point chair, but he'd finished well, and would be able to pay for his hotel room without feeling a pinch.

His lonely hotel room.

Austin felt for the guy. He gave him a nod as he took his place signing autographs, then focused on the fans, who still wanted a signature even though he hadn't come out on top.

He signed and smiled, signed and smiled, ignoring his aching leg. A staff member came up behind him to move some equipment and he half turned to make sure he was out of the way. When he turned back his gaze smacked into a pair of familiar green eyes and the floor felt like it had given way beneath him.

"Kris."

"Yeah." She smiled, but she was nervous, perhaps wondering if she'd made a mistake by appearing out of nowhere to surprise him. Maybe she *had* made a mistake, but that didn't stop him from being glad as hell to see her.

"I'm on my way home from Reno and thought I'd stop by."

"Just…stop by."

"It only added an hour on to my drive time. A quick left turn in Winnemucca and here I am." She stepped aside so that the small line behind her could have their turn with him. After he'd signed his last autograph, he took her hand and led her toward the changing room. Once out of sight he took her face, didn't even consider *not* giving into temptation, and kissed her hard.

"I had to see," she said, bringing her forehead to rest against his chest and exhaling deeply. He wrapped his arms around her a little more tightly.

"See what?"

"Why I can't get you out of my head."

He understood exactly what she was talking about. He

smiled a little then cupped her chin in one hand, tilted up her face, gently kissed her again.

"Hey!" He turned to see Gage heading down the hallway. Austin kept his arms around Kristen as the bull rider walked by.

"Nothing to see here," Austin said to his friend.

"Bet there would be if I hung around."

Austin snorted as Gage disappeared into the changing room. "You want to get out of here?"

"I wouldn't mind being alone with you for a while."

"Wait here while I grab my stuff."

Kristen followed him to his hotel, parked next to him. As soon as they were out of their respective vehicles, he took her hand. It felt right to have her there. Scary right.

But he wasn't going to talk yet. There were other ways to communicate and as soon as the door was closed behind them, he did his best to show how glad he was to see her.

And she seemed equally glad to be with him.

WAS THERE ANYTHING *better than waking up next to a bull rider?*

Well…not just any bull rider. Her bull rider.

Kristen pushed herself up onto one elbow, lightly brushing his hair away from his forehead, one of the few places she was fairly certain wasn't in some way sore. Although…

"You haven't been hit in the head lately?"

"Are you questioning my judgment?"

She laughed. "No. Just checking for safe spots to touch."

He took her hand and laced his fingers with hers, setting their joined hands on his chest. "All parts are safe...within reason."

"Mmm." She stretched out on her side again. "Are you checking out today?"

"Yeah. Going to the Forty-Six to see my brother before he and Shelby head off to Tennessee and I travel south to Cheyenne."

"Your brother is going to Tennessee?"

"He's a technical advisor for another of Buck Creighton's documentaries."

"That's cool."

"Yeah. He fell into a good thing. And it'll keep my dad happy." He pulled her closer and she eased her thigh on top of his, then pulled it back off again. "Stop worrying about hurting me. It's giving me a complex."

"I wasn't worried about it last night." She smiled and raised herself up on her elbow again so that she could see his face. "If I didn't have commitments, I'd go to Cheyenne with you."

He dropped a kiss onto her hair. "Those damned commitments."

"Yes." She smoothed her palm over the hard planes of his chest. "I'm going to ask you for a favor." His muscles tightened ever so slightly beneath her palm, and if her head had been on his chest, she probably would have heard his heart rate kick up. "And please know—I'm saying this more to me than to you. Can we not analyze? Or dissect? Or do any of the things that will bring me crashing back to earth?" She let out a small breath. "I want to enjoy this for a while longer."

Her logical, analytical side always beat down her enjoy-the-feeling side—or it had until Austin came into the picture and gave her that extra incentive to ignore her tight-ass side.

He gave a soft laugh and stroked her hair again, gently twining the strands through his fingers. "Yeah. I can do that. It's kind of what I do."

"Lucky you." She meant that. She was starting to get a feel for what life was like when one didn't second and third-guess every move. She liked the feeling, but was intimidated by it. It was hard to let go on her own, with no one there, like Austin or her twin, to coach her or lead by example. She'd done well making her impulsive side trip to Nampa, but a part of her was still a little rattled that she'd done that...even though it had turned out well.

Very well.

"We can ride as far as Marietta together. I'm pretty sure I can talk Kelly into driving your car if his arm isn't bothering him too much. You can tell me about your interview."

Yes. The interview. She felt as if she was balancing be-tween two worlds—one where she felt safe and knew all the rules, and the other full of unknowns, yet calling to her with a siren's song.

Austin turned his head to meet her gaze, his expression more serious than she expected. "You want to spend some time with me when we get to Marietta? I have a few days to kill before traveling on."

Instead of answering out loud, she slid her palms along the rough planes of his cheeks and pulled his mouth down to hers, then she proceeded to show him, in great detail, why that was the best of ideas.

AUSTIN AND KRISTEN met Kelly for breakfast shortly after Austin and Kristen had shared a rather dynamic shower. They ate at the hotel restaurant, with Austin grabbing the tab for everyone. Kelly's wife hadn't shown, and Austin felt for the guy.

He was also surprised at how Kelly opened up with Kristen, asking her about her plans for the future, and how she felt watching Austin ride bulls.

"Nervous," Kristen said, adding that she really didn't have enough experience to give a definitive answer.

She didn't. She'd watched Austin ride in person three times. Only one of those times had resulted in a wreck, and it had been so minor that it barely qualified.

Once they hit the road, Austin kept clear of the topic of

bull riding, focusing instead on Kristen's remaining time at home and her plans for the future. She was confident she was going to land the job she'd applied for, thanks to some guy she'd worked for in the past.

"I'll do things differently this time," she said. "I wasn't a good team player in the past. I walled myself off too much."

"I find that hard to believe."

She gave him a mock snooty look. "*Someone* helped me tackle that issue, you know. I'm not a full-blown extrovert, but I'm better." The snooty look disappeared, replaced by a smile that lit her eyes, and an odd sensation spread through his chest. She was so damned beautiful.

After dropping Kristen off at her house sooner than he wanted to, Kelly, who'd driven Whitney's little Toyota to Marietta, made noises about renting a car and driving to Cheyenne early.

"Only one problem," Austin said. "No car rental place in Marietta." Kelly's face contorted with frustration, and Austin kind of knew how he felt. "But you can take my truck."

Kelly frowned at him. "How'll you get down there?"

"Borrow a rig from my brother."

"If you're sure."

Austin was sure. If Kelly wanted to head south to see his wife, who was in Fort Collins with her parents, he was going to do everything he could to help the guy.

Kelly dropped Austin at the ranch, which appeared to be deserted. Austin kicked around the kitchen, making himself a sandwich and stealing a beer. Finally he heard boots on the steps, and went to the door, pulling it open for his brother.

"Where is everyone?" he asked.

"Where the hell did you come from?" Ty stepped into the kitchen, taking off his hat and hanging it on the hooks next to the door. He ruffled the back of his hair where the hat had creased it.

"Got dropped off. I loaned my truck to my travel partner."

"And now you want mine?"

"Pretty much."

Ty scowled at him then pushed his chair back and went to the fridge. "Les had a doctor's appointment and Shelby had to drive him because his new medication makes him dizzy as hell." He looked at the empty plate in the sink. "Did you make me a sandwich?"

"No, but I will." Least he could do for the guy who was lending him his truck.

Austin made the sandwich, then joined his brother on the porch, where he set down the plate and picked up the full long neck waiting for him.

Ty propped his feet on the railing and started to eat. "Staying long?"

"I plan to spend some time with Kristen Alexander."

"Ah." Ty chewed in a thoughtful way. "So are you guys getting serious?"

A change of subject was in order, and Austin seized upon

the topic most likely to distract his older brother. "When do I get to find out that I'm going to be an uncle?"

"At the twelve-week mark."

"Which is…?"

"Four more weeks."

"I'll be the first to know…right?"

"You *are* the first to know, however…" he leveled a deadly look at him "…Les will be the 'official' first to know, and he'd better never find out otherwise."

"My lips are sealed. Are you scared?"

"It doesn't seem real yet, but yeah…I'd say I'm kind of intimidated. There's a lot of room to screw up when you're responsible for another life."

Austin smiled to himself. "Are you going to be a stage-dad?" Like their dad.

"Oh, fuck yes. You know I am." Ty tipped up his beer and took an overly long drink.

"Sorry."

Ty snorted. "No, you're not."

He might not be sorry, but he had been successful in sidetracking his brother. Or so he thought until the rooster tail of dust from Shelby's truck showed in the distance as it approached the ranch. "Where's this thing going between you and Kristen?"

"Why do you want to know?"

"I'm just kind of curious."

"Yeah. Me, too." Which was one-hundred-percent true.

"I don't have an answer."

Ty gave a nod, then got up from the chair on the porch and stretched, his eyes on the dusty road as he waited for his wife and grandfather-in-law.

"I know we're kind of an unlikely pair."

"Kind of?" Ty gave his brother a slow look.

Austin sucked in a breath. "There's more to her than meets the eye. A lot more."

"All the same." Ty wrinkled his forehead at him.

Austin's stomach was starting to knot, and there was no reason for it. He'd never sought out his brother's advice when it came to women, and he wasn't about to start now.

Shelby drove into the yard and parked near the cedar fence that bordered the front yard and got out of the truck. Les got out of his side, looking none too happy about having to visit the sawbones again, but when he saw Austin he smiled.

"Got a chore list ready for you. How long are you staying?"

"A few days."

"Excellent." Les took a chair beside Austin as Shelby kissed Ty hello. She told Les she'd bring him ice tea and then she and Ty disappeared into the house. Once inside, Austin could hear them talking, their voices low, the tone intimate.

Shelby and Ty had a lot in common—background, interests, goals. He and Kristen did well together, but what did they have in common? Not too much when one considered lifestyles.

Maybe it isn't about having things in common.

But deep down, he was fairly certain it was.

Chapter Fourteen

THREE DAYS LATER, Austin woke to the sound of someone pounding on the door of his Cheyenne motel room and realized he'd overslept. He'd stayed longer in Marietta than he'd originally planned, wanting one last evening with Kristen before hitting the road for Wyoming.

"Coming," he called as he rolled out of bed and pulled on his jeans. Ten minutes later he and Kelly were on their way to a fast food breakfast.

After a jolt of coffee, he noticed that Kelly seemed to be more upbeat than usual, which was saying something.

"What gives?" Austin asked. "You're almost cheerful."

"Finally heard from Melissa this morning." Kelly smiled a little as he said his wife's name.

"Ah," Austin said. He didn't know much about Kelly's time after he left Marietta, other than the fact that he hadn't been able to hook up with his wife in Fort Collins, because she'd been visiting a sister in Nebraska.

"Yeah." Kelly's smile faded as he picked up his coffee, but he still looked like a different guy. More relaxed. More at peace. Maybe he'd have a happy ending after all. "She's coming to Cheyenne so we can do some talking. We'll drive to Pueblo together."

"That sounds good." Austin didn't mind losing a travel partner who was working things out in his life.

"She wants to have a kid."

Austin's head came up at the announcement, but since he didn't know what to say, he stayed silent.

"The problem is that she won't get pregnant while I'm riding bulls and I can't convince her that this is our best option for getting onto our feet financially."

And let's not forget that you love riding bulls.

Austin focused on his coffee, but couldn't move past the question that pushed itself forward in his brain. "Did she know how much bull riding meant to you when you guys married?"

"I was riding full-time, so yeah. I'd say she had a hint."

"Tough one," Austin said, unwrapping a breakfast sandwich. He'd seen the situation Kelly described in more than one bull-riding relationship. Had seen it play out on a lesser level in his own life.

Kelly dug into his paper bag. "No easy solution, but we'll work things out."

"You think?" The words came out before he thought.

Kelly frowned at him, as if to say "why the fuck are you raining on my parade?" Before Austin could apologize, he said, "Yeah. I do. We love each other."

Austin bit into the sandwich and chewed instead of letting more words fall out of his mouth. As Kelly had said, no easy solution, but Austin wished him the best. He didn't envy him the shit he and his lady had been going through, but it was part of the game. Part of being involved in a difficult career full of uncertainties. A career that every bull rider he knew was grateful to have.

A career *he* was grateful to have.

Could it ever mesh with Kristen's career?

That was the unusual part about being with Kristen these past few days. She'd seemed happy to just be with him, while he, Mr. Here and Now kept wondering about the future.

And he felt comfortable with her. Almost too comfortable.

Belong-together comfortable.

He had no idea how to handle it. No idea where their relationship was going. Kristen didn't want to talk, and his guess was that it was because if they did talk, they'd have to confront hard issues. She wasn't ready for that, probably because it meant facing facts…and it may mean saying goodbye for real instead of letting things get even more serious.

Neither of them were ready for that.

BONNIE ALEXANDER PULLED the teabag out of her cup before leveling a look at her eldest daughter. Things were still a touch stilted between them and Kristen got it. Truly she did. She, the perfect child, the child they never had to worry about, had gone off the rails. She had to rebuild trust, which was a slow process.

"You have no idea when you'll hear for certain about the job?"

"After the other two candidates are interviewed and the committee meets again." She sipped her tea. "But one thing I can promise you—if I go back to Reno, I won't be keeping secrets." No big ones anyway.

"Your life is your own, Kristen." Her mom set down the cup and leaned her forearms on the table, looking like she had something important to say, so Kristen put down her cup, too. "When you told us about your job, I was stunned, because you've never kept anything from us…" Her mom smiled in a reminiscent way. "Well, nothing that someone else didn't tell us."

The joys of living in a small town.

"But after I got over the shock, I was kind of relieved."

"About what?" Kristen asked, shocked.

"You'd finally broken a rule."

Not even close to what she'd thought was coming. "I didn't break a rule. I broke trust."

Her mom smiled a little. "You did. But you also went a little renegade."

Kristen frowned at her.

Her mom reached for her teacup. "Sometimes your perfectionism is over the top. Even for being your father's daughter. It has to be exhausting."

Kristen wanted to argue. Wanted to tell her that she wasn't that much of a perfectionist...but she was. There was no way around that. "Kind of hard to fight one's true nature."

Her mother's expression grew serious. "I know. And I'm not asking you to fight your true nature...I'm just asking you to give yourself a break."

Kristen stared at her own cup, taking in the delicate yellow rose pattern she'd always loved. "I'm not that hard on myself." The words felt like a lie—probably because they were.

She dropped her head back, her hands still on her teacup. Life was so much simpler when her deeply engrained strategies not only worked, but worked well, too. She was at the point now where she didn't know what worked.

Coming up with new strategies was as exhausting as trying to make everything perfect.

Her mom touched her hand and Kristen let go of the teacup and squeezed her mother's fingers. "I'm feeling my way along, Mom. Somewhere along the line, some of the rules changed...or maybe they were never there." Maybe they were all in her head, the 'rules' that helped her conquer each new challenge.

"Tackling life is hard, because it is ever changing. Being rigid helps in some areas, not so much in others."

"Excellent," Kristen said dryly.

Her mother laughed. "I occasionally have this conversation with your father, too."

"But not Whitney?"

Her mom gave a small snort. "No."

Her sister wasn't a perfectionist. She attacked life with more of a let-the-chips-fall-where-they-may attitude that Kristen couldn't help but envy. "I *am* loosening up."

The flat-out truth, however, she would not be sharing Austin's role in the 'loosening' with her mother. Some things were best left unsaid.

"If you can find a middle ground, I think you'll find life less stressful."

Kristen gave a small laugh. "I'll work on it?" She was working on it, but like rebuilding trust it was a slow process.

"Tell me about Austin."

Kristen froze. She hadn't kept the fact that she was keeping company with Austin a secret, but she hadn't expected her mom to ask questions.

"He's good for me," she finally said. "He's teaching me to bend some rules."

Her mother laughed. "Good. Just…don't go overboard. I want you to loosen up, but I don't want two Whitneys on my hands."

AUSTIN FELT GOOD as he eased himself on board Muddy Boy, a shiny dark brown bull with fawn-colored legs and points. A beautiful animal who wanted to do him some serious harm. Nothing new there. Muddy Boy stomped and humped up when the bull rope was tightened. Someone grabbed Austin's vest from behind, spotting him and keeping him in place while he finished his wraps. The bull blew snot, then settled and Austin gave his nod.

In less than a second he was in trouble, thrown off balance by an unexpected sharp twist, just before the spins started, sucking him down into the well. He fought gravity, muscles straining, teeth clenched, then came the rear and twisting buck and it was all over. He hit the ground hard, raised his head and found himself instinctively dodging a hoof. He didn't dodge fast enough and it clipped him, knocking his helmet off. He rolled into a ball as hooves thudded around him, then it got quiet and he chanced a look. Muddy Boy bucked his way to the gate, ignoring the heap of tangled bull rider he'd left in the middle of the arena.

Austin got to his feet and took his helmet from the bull fighter who'd picked it up before he half-walked, half-limped to the gate. Something was running into his eyes and he put his hand to his forehead, felt the blood.

Shit.

Every now and then the bull had to win.

Yeah, yeah, yeah. But this is two in a row.

He was pissed.

Instead of heading to the medical room to get the cut taken care of, he stopped to watch Kelly ride, blood flowing from between his fingers as he put pressure on the cut.

As promised, Kelly's wife had shown up. She was even prettier in person than in the photos Kelly had shown him and she obviously loved her husband. They touched. A lot. Little touches, little strokes on the arm, the hands, the shoulders. Shared smiles. And a strained look on her face when Kelly was otherwise occupied.

She was making a decision. Austin was certain of it, and he could only hope that decision fell in favor of Kelly.

As Kelly mounted the chute where Left of Center was waiting for him, he looked like he could ride a cyclone. In a world where intense concentration was the norm, Kelly was a half-tick past everyone else.

Austin tilted his head back as the gate swung open, working to control the flow of blood, and also ready to catch anything that Kelly might want to know about later. They made it a habit to critique each other's rides, and he didn't want a little blood to keep him from doing that.

The first few seconds went well. Kelly was glued to the center of the bull, anticipating every move. He leaned back into a high twisting buck, his free hand staying well within the plane, then leaned forward as the bull reared, kicking all four feet in the air just before he threw his head back, smacking Kelly square in the forehead.

Kelly's limp body tumbled off the bull on the wrong

side, his hand hanging up in the rigging so that his body flopped beside Left of Center as the bull continued to buck. The bull fighters converged on the animal, one attempting to lure him into a straight line, while the other fought with the rigging. The mounted safety man approached on the offside and managed to catch the flank strap and release it. Left of Center's bucking slowed and the bull fighter managed to lift Kelly to the point that he could ease the weight on his hand, undo the bull rope.

Both bull fighter and bull rider collapsed in the dirt. Only one of them struggled to his feet.

Austin sat back down. Kelly was out cold. At least he hoped he was out cold, and not dead.

His wife is here and she might have just watched her husband die.

The thought made him sick.

The medics and gate personnel crowded around him, making it impossible to see. Then they fell back and Kelly stirred as two medics began moving him onto a backboard. The crowd was quiet as the big gate opened to let the ambulance in and a few long minutes later, it drove out again.

Austin got out of his chair. He needed to find Kelly's wife. Needed to see if she had a way to get to the hospital, because this was not a time for her to drive alone.

KRISTEN WAS IN lying in bed, wide awake and wondering about Austin's ride, which would be televised the following evening, when her phone rang. She scooped it up fast, so it wouldn't wake her sister. Austin. The moment she heard his voice, she knew he hadn't called because he missed her. Something was wrong. Something major.

"Are you all right?" The question came choking out even as she told herself that if he was talking, he was okay.

"I'm fine. It's Kelly."

Kristen closed her eyes, pressing her palm to her forehead. "What happened?" She kept her voice low, so as not to disturb Whitney in the next room.

"Well, he's going to make it."

Austin went on to describe the wreck, and how he'd taken Kelly's wife to the hospital even though he wasn't supposed to leave the venue. Even though there were people who did that, he wouldn't leave her alone.

And Kelly's condition—major concussion, internal injuries, punctured lung, broken arm, dislocated shoulder. There was a laundry list, really, and Austin rattled it off as if those injuries were as familiar to him as items on a fast food menu.

Kristen swallowed hard when he was done and tried to find words. Any words. "I didn't know whether to call you. I...didn't want you to find out via the internet."

"Why *wouldn't* you call me?" Kristen asked.

"I don't know."

She did. Protective instinct was kicking in. Austin was a

protector. It was the reason he wouldn't sleep with her in the beginning.

She pulled in a long breath, swallowed again. "This is awful." An inadequate description of her feelings, however, it was the best she could do. "How are *you*?"

"I've been here before."

Which didn't answer her question. "Austin...?"

"Yeah?" There was a cautious note to his voice, as if he expected her to voice a demand or ask for a promise.

"Maybe I could drive down to Pueblo. Before I get caught up in other things." Other things being the job she still hadn't heard on, although her contact had called to tell her one candidate was definitely out of the running.

"I..."

Her stomach tightened when his voice trailed off. She'd expected him to give her an instant yes.

"I think it would be better if I see you in Marietta after Pueblo."

Her stomach tightened. "You don't want me to come?"

"Not right now."

"Why?" Because everything had been fine between them a few days ago. Better than fine. It'd felt...right.

"It's a long way to drive. I'll be back in a week."

"All right." Not the answer she'd wanted or expected, but she could live with it. He was upset. He'd almost lost a friend tonight. He needed time to come to grips with the situation. "I'll let you know if I land the job."

"I'll see you in a week."

There was something in his tone that she found unsettling.

"See you then." She ended the call before he did and leaned back against the pillows. Closed her eyes. Tried to get a handle on what had just happened. He was upset. And he wanted to be alone while he dealt with matters. She, of all people, the queen of withdrawal, should understand that.

Except she was working double hard *not* to withdraw, and she expected Austin to do the same.

AUSTIN DROPPED AN arm over his eyes after Kristen ended the call. He shouldn't have phoned her tonight. He could have waited until morning, but he'd wanted to hear her voice. To know that she was all right.

Why? He'd made it through many a rough spot in his life without hearing Kristen Alexander's voice. He could have called his brother. Or his father.

No. His dad would have been all over him for a poor ride.

But Ty had been an option. He'd chosen Kristen and had essentially dialed on autopilot as soon as he got back to his room after leaving Melissa Kincaid was with her parents at the hospital. His gut feeling was that after Kelly recovered, he wouldn't be married for long. Melissa kept muttering, "I can't do this," and when her parents arrived from Fort Collins, she'd fallen into her mother's arms, sobbing as if her lungs were going to turn inside out.

Could he do that to Kristen?

That answer to that was an easy 'no'. He never wanted Kristen to go through what Melissa Kincaid was going through, and as he lay staring up through the semi-darkness, the stitches in his head throbbing, he realized why he had called close to midnight—he was hoping to bring her to her senses.

What a chickenshit thing to do. To put the matter in her hands instead of handling it himself. Just as she'd accused him of doing when he wouldn't sleep with her.

Until tonight, he hadn't given a lot of thought as to how his profession might affect the people he cared for, other than in a logistical how-can-our-schedules-mesh way. He'd grown up riding rough stock, as had his father and his brother. His mother had been stoic about injuries—maybe because she'd seen so many. But Melissa Kincaid and Kristen Alexander had not grown up in the business. Broken bones and punctured lungs were not the norm.

He rolled over, pulling the sheet with him, closed his eyes, pictured Melissa's pale, tear-ravaged face.

Who was he to put Kristen in that kind of a position?

He wouldn't do it. He cared for her too damned much.

KRISTEN HAD A week to think after her phone call with Austin. It wasn't hard to deduce what was coming next. They'd known their relationship was temporary from the beginning and now it was waning.

Except that it damned well didn't feel like it was waning—at least not on her end. Not when they were together.

So what now?

She didn't know. It was difficult to prepare when one didn't know what outcome they wanted. If Austin didn't care for her, then yes. Things had to end. It would hurt. A lot. But if he did care...she didn't know.

When Austin's truck finally rolled to a stop in front of her house the day after the Pueblo event, she realized that she wasn't ready to deal with whatever he was about to lay down. The icy calm she relied on to get her through situations like this was nowhere to be found. She felt raw. Naked.

Unable to hide her feelings.

And how terrifying was that? To let Austin see how deeply she'd come to care for him and how much his leaving was going to hurt?

She watched through the living room window as he got out of his truck and started up the walk, hugging her arms to herself. You played. Now you pay.

Right.

She moved toward the door, opened it. Gave her best attempt at a careless smile, which froze when she got a good look at him. Stitches across his forehead. Two black eyes.

Her mouth fell open. "I had no idea."

"Part of the job." He spoke coolly, dashing her last remaining hope that she might have read things wrong. He wasn't there to connect. He was there to disconnect.

She swallowed as she took in his battered face.

You are strong.

Yes, she was. And she wasn't going to address his injury. She knew how it happened; she simply hadn't known the extent of the damage. He was on his feet, and that was all that mattered in that regard. His injuries were not why he was there.

"Are you here to end things?" It made sense to cut to the chase.

Austin seemed startled by the question, but he regrouped quickly. "It's what I have to do."

"Why?"

"I think you know the answer, Kristen. All parts of it."

She dipped her chin. Seven days of analysis had given her a firm base upon which to build. His mouth flattened as he jammed a thumb into his front pocket. "I enjoyed our time together."

Really, Austin? Could you sound any more distantly polite? That's my gig.

"It's ending rather abruptly."

"It needs to. Before it goes too far."

"Could it? Go too far?"

His expression blanked out in a way she hadn't seen before. She wasn't the only one with a protective barrier.

She stepped toward the window, giving herself some space as her mind worked. She looked back at him. "What is too far?"

"Too far is when someone can get hurt. Not breakup hurt, but life-altering hurt."

Her brows pulled together. "I…don't understand."

"We could spend a lot of time debating this, but the bottom line is that our lives are different. Our goals are different. We are different."

"And you're falling in love with me." Kristen had no idea where she'd gotten the strength to toss that out there, but there it lay, like a live bomb between them.

Austin's blue gaze drilled into her. "Maybe that's the biggest reason." So much for the bomb. Dealt with and now what?

She wanted to reach out and take him by the front of the shirt. Shake some sense into him. If he loved her, then…

Nothing. Because it always came back to the same issue. Austin's forte.

"Who are you protecting?"

"You." The word came out of his mouth almost before her question was asked. "And that's just the way it is." The thumb hooked in his pocket dragged it down even more. "This isn't easy for me, Kris. But it is realistic."

Realistic. She disagreed. If it was realistic, she wouldn't be fighting it so much. *She* was the realist of the two. She started to hug her arms around herself, then quickly dropped them to her sides, opening herself back up. She refused to look defensive. Or hurt. He knew she was hurt. No sense belaboring the point.

"This is for the best, Kristen."

"Right. Got another platitude?"

His mouth tightened. They were four feet apart, but it felt like a mile. A gulf separated them that didn't have to be there.

"When you left Marietta, things were good between us. What changed?"

"I guess I just came to my senses."

She let out an exasperated breath. "You're afraid that if you give me the real reason, that I'll figure a way around it."

The shift in his expression confirmed her suspicion. He wasn't about to give her more ammo, which meant that he was worried about what she might do with it. "It doesn't matter if you do, Kristen. We need to end things. Now." Austin shifted his weight. "I should go."

No. You should stay here and duke this out with me.

Was his sudden retreat tied to his injury? The stitches, the black eyes, the fractured leg?

Her gut told her no. It was connected to his friend's injury—or maybe it was the result of a perfect storm of circumstances. The one thing she did know was that he believed he was doing the right thing, standing here, breaking her heart.

They would address that later, after she had time to think.

He started for the door and she realized that she couldn't let him leave thinking that this was over.

"I'm tougher than you're giving me credit for, Austin."

He turned at the door, his intense blue gaze zeroing in on her. "And sometimes we're not as tough as we think." His mouth tightened. "That's when we break."

SMOOTH, HARDING. VERY smooth.

Austin felt like shit as he drove away from Kristen's house, but he'd done the right thing. How could it not be the right thing if it saved Kristen grief in the end?

Maybe, you jerk, she would have just forgotten you after moving to Reno. Maybe circumstances would have gotten in the way and you guys would have drifted apart.

And maybe that was yet another chickenshit way to handle things.

This way there was no question about their relationship. It was over.

Austin ran his fingers over the stitches, testing the area for tenderness. A reminder of their different worlds. They weren't even supposed to have a relationship. Kristen had wanted to break free of her self-imposed rules and regulations. He'd wanted to help her because he'd sensed there was someone he could like beneath her coolly defensive exterior.

Oh, he'd liked her all right. A little too much.

And she likes you.

Therein lay the problem, because how in the hell was she supposed to work her life around his? He couldn't think of a way without her giving up something significant. Something she would regret giving up later. And there wasn't a question of him giving up his life—he had nothing to fall back on. No plan. Which was starting to look like it might develop into an issue. It wasn't like he could be Les Connor's grunt on the Forty-Six Ranch forever. The guy worked him because he enjoyed working him, not because they were falling behind in upkeep and maintenance. Shelby and Ty kept the place up just fine. They didn't need help.

If he was in Kelly's shoes, what in the hell would he do in the long term?

Another tick in the 'you did the right thing with Kristen' column.

All the ticks were there. Once she cooled off, Kristen would realize that. She was logical. Sensible.

Intuitive, funny, supportive. Sexy.

Stop.

Austin turned onto the road leading to the Forty-Six. He'd grab his gear and take a nice slow drive to Omaha. He'd made plans to stop at a bull-riding practice pen owned by a friend in Rapid City and another in Sioux City. If he could find other pens along the way, he'd stop at them, too.

And maybe he should give thought to his post bull-riding career while he had some time alone on the road—although focusing on the future might just mess with his present. Mess with his focus. He was a bull rider. And when he wasn't, he wasn't.

The future would be there no matter what he did now.

One thing was for certain, though—he was going to face that future alone until he had something worthy to share.

THE CALL FROM Reno came ten days after Austin had disappeared from Kristen's life. Ten hellish days in which she'd weighed pros versus cons, sensible decisions versus impulsive decisions. Reality versus fantasy.

Reality got a foothold when she was told she had the job.

She let out a long breath, overwhelmed by a feeling of sheer relief. Security was only a couple signatures away. She'd be leaving Marietta, picking up her life in Reno. Continuing on her chosen path, wiser in the ways of the corporate world, and no longer naïve enough to believe that hard work guaranteed success.

They needed an answer by Monday, which gave her the weekend. She could say yes right now. Give a verbal, settle the matter.

She wasn't ready to do that, and the fact that she hesitated gave her pause. *Was fantasy winning?*

Or did she not want to look too damned desperate?

Kristen didn't know, and the fact that she hadn't given an instant verbal told her that she had a lot to think about. "Thank you. I'll get back to you on Monday. Do I call you personally?"

"Yes. You have my extension, right?"

"Right. I'll talk to you then."

After hanging up the phone, Kristen did not do a happy dance. She idly rubbed her upper arms as she paced through the war room. Why hadn't she jumped immediately?

What was the reason?

Her parents and sister and Marietta came to mind, but the real reason was nearly a thousand miles away, going about his business, riding bulls and putting his life on the line.

Protecting her.

Who was protecting him?

Sometimes we aren't as tough as we think we are. That's when we break.

Break, indeed.

KELLY KINCAID WOULD never again ride bulls, and he was also on the road to divorce. Double whammy. Austin told himself that it wasn't his business, but Kelly's situation ate at him. The guy had been so in love. And Melissa had appeared to love him, too.

But maybe not enough.

"Or maybe too much," Shelby pointed out when she and Ty stopped in Omaha to watch him ride while on their way to Tennessee and he filled them in about his friend. "And you don't know what went on with them. Sometimes guys aren't good at reading the signs. And sometimes they ignore the signs."

Well, he wasn't guilty of that. He'd read the signs and deduced that he wasn't going to put Kristen through hell. A little pain now was better than a lot of pain later. From what he'd been able to glean from the Marietta grapevine, she'd landed her job in Reno. Once there, she'd slide back into her old life, hook up with some guy who didn't regularly flirt with death and all would be well.

For both of them.

He had to remember that, but sometimes it was hard when he was dealing with a hole in his gut that wasn't diminishing with time.

You're doing the right thing—doing what you have *to do.*

He couldn't offer Kristen the security she needed, couldn't even guarantee that he'd have a job in a year, a month, a week. If he got hurt tomorrow, if he found himself in Kelly Kincaid's shoes, he had no backup plan, other than holing up on the Forty-Six until he figured out his plan.

Whatever that might be. The practice pens he'd visited had been inspiring, but he'd need a partner to set one up.

And a clientele. And a location. Even if he had all those things, the reality was that he'd probably still need a day job to make ends meet. That meant luck or training.

He missed the days when he hadn't thought about the future.

Missed them a lot.

He did his best to focus on his upcoming ride as he traveled north on Highway 93. It was late afternoon when Missoula came into view, the city spreading out in the valley beneath the mountains that had once held a deep glacial lake. He'd always liked Missoula. He'd had some good times there. He planned to have more good times.

While he could.

Austin's face tightened. He had to stop thinking like that. It wasn't doing his rides any good. He'd finished okay in Omaha, okay in Deadwood, okay in Billings. But he'd dropped a couple places in the standings and needed to ramp up his focus. Regain lost ground.

Missoula was where he was going to do that. If nothing else, he'd do it for Kelly, the guy who'd helped him see that no matter how much you might want something, that didn't mean you were going to get it.

Chapter Fifteen

S LICK BACK WAS a small bull with a nasty attitude—quick and agile, totally unpredictable. There would be no lazy spins or half-hearted bucks. Slick Back relished every contest, and Austin had been fortunate to draw him when he needed a high score to boost his standings. The bull would do his part. It was all on Austin now.

The bull shifted nervously, stamping his feet as Austin went through his prep. As soon as he was in place, Austin nodded. The spotter released his vest and Slick Back burst out into the arena before the gate fully opened, snapping Austin's head back with the force of his first landing.

Austin tucked his chin, pushed down hard, rolled a shoulder first in, then out, to counteract a sudden spin followed by an equally sudden reversal. The bull's feet pounded the earth, but he still moved fluidly, his back humping as he pushed his shoulders high into the air, all four feet coming off the ground. He landed hard, swinging his ass around, pounding the arena floor again as he reared, then spun. Austin stayed square in the middle, sheer determination holding him in place at times. The horn sounded and he started debating dismounts, when suddenly Slick Back shifted beneath him, shifted in a way that his body hadn't expected and the world went sideways as the bull's feet came out from under him and he slammed to the ground on his side, taking Austin with him.

The blackness started to clear, giving way to a mottled black and white world as Austin opened his eyes, inhaled dirt. He tried to lift his head, but pressure from above kept it from moving.

Pinned. He was pinned under the bull. He had to get free.

He put his palms in the dirt, pushed up. Couldn't move. The weight was too great. Frantic now, he pulled his knee up to get it under him so that he could struggle free of the massive bull and his body exploded in pain. An animalistic sound ripped out of his throat.

"It's me, buddy. You're okay. Lie still."

Austin didn't recognize the voice, but his brain started to wrap around the fact that it wasn't the bull that had him pinned. Slick Back wasn't lying on him. He was being held down by a fellow human being. Kept from moving. *Why?*

He wasn't paralyzed. The pain was too fucking intense. But he needed to get to the gate before the bull came back.

He couldn't move.

His head went back down; he took another lungful of dirt. Closed his eyes. Moaned again.

"Easy."

There were hands on him. Testing, touching. Voices. A

low rumble. Not a bull. An engine. A vehicle. He was going to be run over if he didn't get off the highway he was lying on. He struggled again and was rolled over onto something hard. Pinned down again as he squinted against the bright orbs of light above him.

And then he was weightless. Rising in the air. Moving.

Ambulance. They were putting him in a fucking ambulance.

Better than lying on a highway waiting to be run over. Maybe.

A face came into focus. One of the medical guys, peering down at him, looking concerned. Too concerned.

Austin made a sound and the guy leaned closer.

"Score?" The word slurred out of his lips, barely audible, but the guy understood.

"Ninety something, man. You did good."

KRISTEN'S HEAD CAME up at the sound of footsteps in the deserted hospital corridor, and she rose to her feet as a nurse came around the corner, clipboard in hand. The nurse gave Kristen an encouraging smile. "You can go in now."

"Thank you." The words barely came out. Despite several cups of coffee, her throat was dry, her nerves shot.

"He's on serious pain meds. He may not remember this visit."

"I just want to see him." She'd driven almost four hours from Marietta to Missoula without stopping, arriving at the hospital in the early hours of the morning, only to be told that Austin was still in recovery.

That was when she started pacing. Pacing and making serious life choices. There was no way that Austin was going through this alone. His brother and sister-in-law were in Tennessee. His parents in Arizona. She was available and when Shelby Harding had called her to tell her that Austin had a bad wreck, she hadn't even paused to pack a bag. She'd grabbed her jacket, purse and keys and headed out the door. It wasn't until she got to Missoula that she'd sent her sister a text telling her that her car hadn't been stolen. It was in Missoula.

"Room 544. Almost to the end of the hall, on the right."

Kristen thanked the nurse and started down the corridor, needing more than anything to confirm that Austin was in one piece.

He's alive. He's okay. It could have been worse.

She'd repeated the words so many times that they blurred together in her head, had essentially lost meaning, but still made her feel better. The door was open when she reached the room and she paused before going inside. His eyes were shut, his skin pale, his hair sticking out in random spikes against the pristine pillow. There was a nasty abrasion up one side of his face, another on his sinewy forearm, which rested atop the white sheet covering his lower body.

Kristen walked toward the bed, coming to a stop a few feet away, giving herself time to process the extent of Austin's injuries. The adrenaline that had kept her going for the past six hours was dissipating, leaving her feeling weak. Exhausted. And close to tears.

She could cry later. When she was alone.

She dropped her purse on the counter and was about to take a seat in the chair next to the bed when Austin's eyes opened. He frowned as he fought to focus, making her wonder if he thought she was some kind of a drug-induced hallucination.

"Why are you here?" The words croaked out of his dry lips.

Would he remember this conversation in the morning?

Judging from his almost fully dilated pupils, she guessed the answer was no. But if he did remember, he'd be chewing on the truth. "Shelby called."

Another slow-motion frown formed as he digested that bit of information. "Shelb?"

"Yeah."

His eyes drifted shut again, a grimace of pain forming on his face. "Why?"

She could barely hear him, so she moved closer. "Maybe she figured out something you didn't."

It took him a few seconds to say, "What?"

"We'll talk about that later." At length.

His thumb clicked the medication button he held in one

hand and then his hand relaxed. He'd drifted off again…or so Kristen thought, until he said her name.

She moved closer to the bed, fighting the urge to touch him. Feel the warm of this body, the reassuring beat of his heart under her hand. "Yes?"

Austin pulled in a deep breath, his face contorting as his chest rose. He exhaled painfully, then whispered, "You shouldn't be here."

Kristen had expected the rejection. Had steeled herself for it.

It still stung.

She gave her head a weary shake. "But I am here."

And there wasn't a lot Austin could do about it.

IT WAS THE scent that tugged at him, urging him to surface, to open his eyes. Delicately floral with just a hint of something else. Some kind of spice. Kristen's scent.

As soon as he came fully conscious, Austin rolled his head to the side, fully expecting to find her sitting next to him, but the chair beside the bed was empty. Marshaling his strength, he lifted his head. The bathroom door was open. The curtains that divided the room were pushed to the wall.

There was no one in the room.

But she'd been there. He was certain of it.

He fumbled for the medication pump and found that it

was gone. Probably a good thing. His leg, his entire lower body, ached like a son of a bitch, but he wanted a clear head as he dealt with this new wrinkle in his life.

He slowly lifted the sheet to take a look at his lower body. His right leg was wrapped and when he shifted it even minutely, he could feel trouble brewing. His right hip hurt like hell, his right shoulder didn't want to move and he could feel the bruise throbbing on that side of his face. The nurse came in during his once-over, introduced herself as Dani, and made him tell her his name and birthdate before setting about making him more comfortable. As if that were even a possibility. "Want to give me a rundown on what all they did to me last night?"

She smiled. "The bull or the doctor?"

"Let's go with the doctor."

"Looks like you have a rod in your lower leg, and other than that, bruising and swelling. A minor concussion. You got off lightly from what I hear."

Her description sounded so cut and dried. Rod in leg. Bruising. Swelling. She didn't mention the part where he felt like he was coming apart, both physically and mentally. Why did the room smell like Kristen?

"Was there a woman here last night?" he asked Dani as she made notations on the white board hanging opposite his bed. "Long reddish hair?" *Beautiful?*

Dani gave him a regretful smile. "I came on shift at seven."

"Thanks."

Dani moved on to her next patient, leaving Austin stared up at the ceiling wondering if he was imagining things. It seemed so real, the scent, but maybe it wasn't.

He drifted off again, only to be startled awake by a hand on his arm. His eyes jerked open and he found himself staring blankly at the man standing next to his bed who wore green scrubs and a pleasant expression.

"Expecting someone else?" the doctor asked with a half-smile before extending a hand. "Adam Medina. You may not remember me from last night. I put your leg back together."

"Thank you."

The doctor went on to describe the procedure and after-care, but he didn't answer the one question Austin wanted answered. "Do you think I'll be able to make any more events this season?"

"Normally I'd say no. But you're a bull rider."

Austin gave a small choking laugh. It hurt.

"Let's take this a day at a time for a while. See how you mend. I've already been in consultation with one of my colleagues in Bozeman." He checked his clipboard, then looked back at Austin. "If you plan to return to Marietta, that is. That's what we have as a permanent address."

"I am." He had nowhere else to go.

"If you're agreeable, he'll handle the follow-ups."

"I don't see myself driving to Missoula."

"Kind of what I figured."

Austin closed his eyes, grimaced in spite of his intention not to. There wasn't a place on his body that didn't ache.

"Doing okay with the pain?" the doctor asked.

"It's an old friend."

"This is probably like an old friend and a lot of his relatives."

Austin smiled instead of laughing. Even that hurt. "I'll take whatever doesn't mess with my head."

"I'll see that you get something to take the edge off, but for the most part you'll have to muscle through if we don't mess with your head."

He finished his exam, made a few notes and was about to leave when Austin asked, "Have you seen a woman with long reddish hair hanging around out there?"

The doctor shook his head. "Sorry. I haven't."

"Thank you." Once the doctor left, Austin stared up at the ceiling. Maybe he really had imagined that Kristen was with him the night before. Maybe he'd wanted her to be with him so badly that he'd conjured her up. Had a conversation with her.

His eyebrows came together as vague images teased the edges of his memory. Something about telling her she shouldn't be there. It seemed real...but his concussed brain could have been hallucinating. Addressing his memory of Kristen. Asking her to leave so that he could stop thinking about her. Like that was going to happen.

He was losing it.

His body was beat to shit, his career was in limbo, he had no backup plan to speak of, and he was hallucinating about the woman he'd accidentally fallen in love with. He didn't need a pain medication that messed with his head. He was doing just fine in that regard on his own.

AUSTIN WAS ASLEEP when Kristen arrived back at his room. She'd checked into a motel and purposely waited until just after noon to come back to the hospital, hoping he would be lucid. During that time, she'd slept, showered and been in contact with his brother who'd called the hospital early that morning. The bull had splintered Austin's tibia, wrenched his knee, bruised the hell out of him and given him a concussion. When he was finished explaining the injuries, Ty had assured Kristen that Austin was tough as hell. These injuries might slow him down, but they wouldn't put him out.

Kristen knew about Austin being tough as hell, and she also knew about him being stubborn as hell. It was the stubbornness she was there to deal with today.

His eyes opened as she came into the room, slowly at first, as if he was getting his bearings, but as soon as he saw her standing in the doorway, his gaze sharpened.

"Kris."

"Yeah." She moved closer to the bed. "You're looking better."

"Better than what?"

Better than a big hole in my life. "Better than you did the last time I saw you."

"You were here last night." A flat statement of fact, but spoken in a way that told Kristen that he couldn't remember what had happened while he was under the influence of the pain meds.

"I was."

"We talked."

"We did. You told me I shouldn't be here."

"I had a good point."

She simply shook her head. "You didn't."

His mouth flattened briefly as he held her gaze, but Kristen remained stubbornly silent. If she didn't say anything, he couldn't argue.

"How did you find out about my wreck?" he finally asked.

"Your sister-in-law called me as soon as they got word."

"Shelby." Austin pressed his hand over his forehead as if he had a sudden headache.

"She called and I started driving."

He dropped his hand back to the sheets, drilled her with a hard look edged with something else. "Why?"

She studied him instead of forming an immediate answer, taking in his pale, beat-up face, spiky hair, the scruff covering his cheeks and angular jaw, which gave him a sexy unkempt look, if one ignored the big abrasion and the bruise that was starting to bloom under one eye. "You know why."

"Damn it, Kris."

"Austin…" His name came out softly, almost as a plea.

He reached out his hand, almost as if he couldn't help himself and she came closer, slipped her fingers into his. His grip tightened as if he was willing her to understand what he was about to say. "I have no job, Kris. I have no way to pay my bills other than tap into my savings."

"I don't have a job either, so I guess we have that in common."

His gaze went dark. "What happened to Reno?"

"I turned it down."

"You're killing me, Kris."

She let out a small choked laugh, feeling like she was on the edge of losing it, but needing to hold it together to get a toe hold in this battle of wills. She gained a measure of strength from the fact that he hadn't let go of her hand.

"We have something else in common. You're killing me, too."

"That's not my intention."

"I know your intentions." She pulled her hand out of his and took a step away from the bed, out of reach. "You know how much my life changed after we got together—for the better. I started thinking in ways that I never thought I could. I started looking at life differently. But you…" She glanced down at the tile floor as she tried to find the words to express her frustration. "You have this stubborn idea in your head about protecting others, about protecting *me*. But you're not protecting me—you're hurting me."

"Kris—"

"It's true, and it's not necessary. If *I* was the one lying in that bed, where would you be?" When he didn't say anything, she took a chance and answered for him. "I think you would be right where I am. I think you would miss a bull-riding event if I was in that bed and needed you."

Austin exhaled. "Yeah, I probably would."

"Then why is it any different for me to be here?"

"Probability. You don't do life-threatening things on a weekly basis, so the chances of me being in your shoes are slim."

"I can accept that you have a greater probability of risk."

"You say that now."

"Austin…how long are you going to be able to ride bulls?" She could see he didn't like that question, but she forged on anyway. "I can last as long as you can. Your job is part of the package. I am not Kelly Kincaid's wife, or any of your past girlfriends who couldn't handle what you do."

"You might have to last for years." The word came out on a low, intense note, giving her a stirring of hope.

"Do you love me?" For the second time in her life she tossed the ultimate question in front of Austin. For the second time, she held her breath until she heard the answer.

"You know I do." There was a rawness in his voice that touched something deep, deep inside of her. She knew that rawness. Knew it well.

"Then I shouldn't have to beg to be part of your life."

"I don't want you to beg." He looked startled at the thought.

"Good. Because I'm not going to." She swallowed, considered just how close to lying she was, then lifted her hand, her thumb and forefinger separated by a tiny fraction of an inch. "But I might come close."

Austin reached out and took her hand again, tugged her closer to the bed with a surprising show of strength. "You'll never beg with me," he said. "If I can give it to you, you will have it."

Kristen's lips parted as she stared down at the battered, sexy guy she loved so much. "I want you."

For a long, tense moment, she thought he was going to turn her down, serve up rejection number three. Instead, he let go of her fingers and ran his hand up her arm, easing her toward him. She lost her balance as she bent over the bed, but managed to catch her weight with her free hand, before he pulled her mouth to his.

Home. She'd come home.

She let out a soft sigh and pulled back.

"I don't want to hurt you."

"Avoid my entire right side," he muttered before meeting her lips again, kissing her as if he was trying to make up for all the hurt he'd caused. Kissing her as if he couldn't imagine life without her.

It wasn't until she touched his face he said, "You could have anyone, Kris. You could have a normal life."

"I want you. Scars, abrasions, broken legs, dangerous occupation. I want it all."

It was awkward bending over him, half on, half off the bed. She would have loved to stretch out beside him, but was scared to death of jarring his broken leg. Part of the deal she'd signed on for. She could do it.

"You know," he said quietly as he smoothed the hair away from her face. "I really might be a loser now. I didn't prepare for the future because I figured it would just be me. I didn't count on you coming into my life."

She let her head rest on the pillow next to his. "You'll never be a loser, Austin. And we can work out the future together. It's scary leaving the beaten path, but the rewards are many for those who dare."

He smiled into her eyes. "Lofty thought."

She gave a low laugh before lightly kissing his perfect lips. "We're going to do okay, Harding. We really are."

Epilogue

AUSTIN'S CLOSE ENCOUNTER with Slick Back ultimately caused him to miss the remainder of the season. He'd willed his leg to heal, and it did—but not fast enough. Finally he'd decided that he'd rather go into the next season at one hundred percent, than salvage what remained of the current one.

Besides that, for the first time in forever, he had something else to focus on. Something worthwhile that made him feel like coming home—and he actually had a home. He and Kristen had set up a single-wide trailer on the Forty-Six Ranch, thus making Les O'Connor a happy man because now he could work Austin whenever he felt like it.

Kristen didn't officially live on the Forty-Six, and wouldn't until they tied the knot in December—just before the season started—but she spent most of her time there, helping Austin with his rehab, working on her new business, and just generally making him feel grateful as hell that she'd been more stubborn than him.

Damn but he loved that woman.

His ice princess.

"Hey…" Kristen wandered into the spare bedroom they used as an office—she to run her new bookkeeping business and he to take online classes in preparation for his post bull-riding career in education. He didn't know yet if he was going to open a bull-riding school, or follow Teller's path and work in some kind of counseling, but he was going to get a degree. Face the future with a plan in place.

Kristen set some knitting down in front of him, pushing her hair back as she said, "Can you see the mistake?"

Austin took a long look at what was eventually going to be a sweater for Ty and Shelby's baby and shook his head. "No."

"Then I guess I can ignore it, rather than taking out all those rows?"

He hooked an arm around her waist and pulled her closer. "Do not pull out rows." She leaned into him, smiled a little as she reached for the needles. He caught her hand, brought it to his lips as his hand slid down to her ass.

"I haven't stretched today."

"Yeah?" A slow smile curved her beautiful lips.

"Or done my exercises."

"Hmmm."

"Want to give me a hand with my rehabilitation?"

She leaned down to give him a long, slow kiss. "I'm always up for some rehab. That's why I hooked up with a bull rider."

He gave a low laugh and pulled her down onto his lap.

"The bull rider appreciates the help." His expression became more serious as he added, "With everything."

She touched her forehead to his, the gesture feeling almost as intimate as a kiss. "Then I guess I also need to say thank you for changing my life."

"It wasn't easy. You fought me at every turn."

Kristen leaned back, her sudden frown belying the amusement in her eyes. "Right. That's exactly how I remember it, too. No stubborn man trying to save me from what I wanted more than anything."

He gave a small shrug. "It seemed the thing to do at the time." He smiled then and brought his hand up to stroke the side of her face. "I love you, Kris. Always have, always will."

She smiled back in a way that made him believe that if a woman like her loved him, then all things were possible. "Likewise, Austin. I love you, too."

The End

The American Extreme Bull Riders Tour

If you enjoyed *Austin*, you'll love the rest of the American Extreme Bull Riders Tour!

Book 1: *Tanner* by Sarah Mayberry

Book 2: *Chase* by Barbara Dunlop

Book 3: *Casey* by Kelly Hunter

Book 4: *Cody* by Megan Crane

Book 5: *Troy* by Amy Andrews

Book 6: *Kane* by Sinclair Jayne

Book 7: *Austin* by Jeannie Watt

Book 8: *Gage* by Katherine Garbera

About the Author

Jeannie Watt is the author of over 20 contemporary romances and the recipient of the Holt Medallion Award of Merit. She lives in a small ranching community—a place where kids really do grow up to be cowboys—with her husband, dog, cat, horses and ponies. When she's not writing, Jeannie enjoys sewing retro fashions, running, and buying lots and lots of hay.

If you'd like to know more about Jeannie, check out her website JeannieWatt.com.

Thank you for reading

Austin

If you enjoyed this book, you can find more from all our great authors at TulePublishing.com, or from your favorite online retailer.

TULE
PUBLISHING

Printed in Great Britain
by Amazon

10127329R00153